Missouri's Memories

The Time Travels of
Annie Sesstry

Book Two

BRENDA WELBURN

To My Mother Alone

We are the chosen. In each family there is one who seems called to find the ancestors—to put flesh on their bones and make them live again, to tell the family story and to feel that somehow, they know and approve.

To me, doing genealogy is not a cold gathering of facts but, instead, breathing life into all who have gone before.

We are the story tellers of the tribe. All tribes have one.

We have been called by our genes. Those who have gone before cry out to us: tell our story. So, we do. In finding them, we somehow find ourselves.

The Genealogy Poem by Della M. Cummings, 1943
Edited and reworded by Tom Dunn, 1943

Contents

Introduction

S*ly as a Fox* launched *The Time Travels of Annie Sesstry*, the fictionalized tale of Lavern "Fox" McElmurry, the first traceable ancestor of the McElmurry-Calhoun Family. Picking up where *Sly as a Fox* leaves off, *Missouri's Memories* is the second in the trilogy of the *Time Travels of Annie Sesstry*, advancing the family beyond Reconstruction into the twentieth century.

As research on the history of the McElmurry-Calhoun family and their descendants progressed, new information emerged. The author amended the spelling of McElmurry from the first book, reflecting what is recorded most frequently in public records and used by other branches of the family. Joshua and Missouri's descendants used the spelling "MacElmurry"; however, the consistency of the spelling in records prescribed the change.

Despite minor revisions from the first book, *Missouri's Memories* stays true to the author's insight of her family's story described by her mother and other family members. In contrast to the first book, this story includes more information accessible from established and often-told family stories and history. Some elements of the story in the book take place at different times from the actual events. However, it does not alter the context of the story or the significance of the event. For example, in the book, the exchange between Joshua Calhoun and the prison warden Troy Raines regarding the men on the chain gang happens on the night Mamie goes into labor with her fourth child.

In fact, that child, the author's mother, was old enough to witness the daily procession of the chain gang convicts, overhear the conversation between Raines and her grandfather and understand its implications. It troubled her because the prisoner Raines spoke of was not among the detainees two days after the exchange between the two men nor was he ever seen again. She suspects Raines killed at least one of the prisoners on the chain gang for which he had oversight.

Lastly, it is significant to note that the family generally refers to itself as the Calhoun-McElmurry family or descendants. The author consciously reversed the names given that Fox McElmurry is the first recognized ancestor and his daughter Missouri, the first matriarch since there is limited knowledge of Fox's wife, Mary. The decision to recount this installment of the family story through Missouri McElmurry Calhoun's experiences challenges the tradition that the Calhoun/McElmurry descendants' success is attributable primarily to Joshua Calhoun.

Research strongly suggests that Missouri was committed to the idea of educating her children and encouraged them to go as far as possible. At the time of the marriage between Missouri and Joshua, Missouri could read, Joshua could not, making his mark on legal documents. Later documents reflect he received some education, learning to read and write after their union. It is conceivable, Missouri was his teacher. It is plausible that his success as a businessman was partly due to his wife's strength, grace, and intelligence.

Missouri was the foundation holding her family and frequently her community together in challenging times. This book celebrates the course she laid out for her children and her family. In the spirit of the Sankofa, we continue to reach back for what may have been forgotten—the contributions of our foremothers.

Prologue

My death was insignificant. It merely marked the passing of an old and now useless slave. The tyrants bred my replacement the same way they raised livestock. Their system insured my proxy. Such was the story of my predecessors. Without fail, it would be the fate of future generations. Each one supplanted by another until blood is shed in the name of freedom.

In their shallowness, the enslavers failed to recognize or acknowledge my incalculable worth. Their arrogant hearts demurred from the stark truth conspicuous before their eyes. They enslaved my body; but I was never a slave. They never owned me. By no means did they hold sway over my spirit. Every individual captive forcefully brought to this territory under duress, was unique. Crafted by the hands of the Creator, we possessed sharp minds, strong bodies, and immortal souls.

The captors ignored an elemental reality; seizing me and others such as me, ripping multitudes from our native land was an abomination. Accordingly, their actions will not be without consequences. There will be a hefty price to pay for their moral depravity. They persist in ignorance of the mighty and righteous power released by their actions. It is a power born from the pain of a stolen people in a stolen land. It is a smoldering ember that cannot be extinguished by an indifferent and heartless captor. They planted a seed of bitterness and nurtured it in the soil of violence and degradation. It will chafe for generations; though, new life and new hope will sprout. Greed cursed a nation with division *and disaffection. But it set into motion a determination for survival in these people that cannot be deterred.*

My body expired and turned to dust. But my soul lingered in Sasha, the limbo between life and death. The journey to Zamani cannot be completed until the natural order is restored and what was taken from me, and my countrymen and women is redeemed. I am at rest, but not at peace. My spirit lives on in my descendants. It lives to guide them. It lives to demand justice and recognition. And like the spirits of all Unknowns, my essence resides at every intersection of this nation. It is fierce. The former enslavers sense it, and strive, though fail, to repress it. Despite their best efforts, they cannot blindly divert their attention away from the hardened faces that remind them of past and present sins. They cannot evade the curled angry fists of the weathered hands that built a nation. Fists that will one day stretch toward an unblemished sky in protest.

The Unknown Ancestors weep silent tears. We are witnesses to the human wreckage spawned by the enslavers when captivity ends. Slavers no longer hold the people in bondage by law, but bleak circumstances fuel exploitation. Oppression continues. The evil ones have not altered their ways. They are determined to rule this Black and mulatto race forever. Landowners control the feigned freedom of Black people who remain tethered to the fields, laboring to stretch out a meager existence. They work as sharecroppers, housekeepers, craftsmen, and traders. Emulating earlier times, the workers are indebted to the landowners who hold their subsistence in their hands. The proprietors control how these freed men feed their families. They regulate their survival, and thus render them impotent from day to day.

But my bloodline, my descendants shall not be cowed. They are sur-vivors. They have strength. Having learned a potent lesson from the sla-vers, they comprehend a significant truth. In property, there is power, in the land there is freedom. It is not enough to work the land or live off the land of others. They discern they must have their own property to prosper. It will begin with a few acres and increase to hundreds more; not by an unfulfilled promise of forty acres and a mule gifted by an indifferent government. It will be acreage earned through hard work and sacrifice.

They will hold the land until the great migration, when the younger generations will depart in search of a different life, a perceived better life.

Their property will slowly slip away. But perseverance and determination will continue to drive them, and they will find freedom and success in alternative ways. Yet, even in that success, they will be scorned and tormented by lesser men.

The migration will have its price. It will cost the people, not just the land, but also their ancestral history. Their knowledge of the past will fade as they struggle for survival. Bygone times will be a vague memory. Some will forget the past. Others will never grasp its true meaning. Some who are familiar with the history will deliberately bury the stock-piled memories passed on to them by the elders. They will find such memories too painful to speak of and carry forward. They will leave stories untold; stories of exploited people, victimized by a painful past they struggle to forget, bearing a shame, not of their own making. But with heartbreaking tales, stories of triumph and survival will also be lost. And the brothers and sisters will be witnesses to others rewriting who and what they are.

Nevertheless, the resolve of the Unknown Ancestors will not allow the false narrative to prevail. We will recast our story in truth. We will restore our people's knowledge. We will give truth to power, for as the African proverb states "at the bottom of patience one finds heaven."

The children will be our messengers. In their innocence, they will accept the impossible. They will travel across generations and tell their family stories. My descendant scion will tell the story of the land and the legend of the man and woman who construct the memoirs of the McElmurry/Calhoun clan.

Chapter 1

Dreams and Nightmares

Annie sprinted towards the woods, slamming into a thick briar. Clawing her way through the brush, she ignored the thorns piercing her hands and the branches tugging her mangled curls. Sweat soaked through the heavy woolen skirt and high-necked blouse. The Edwardian laced boots did not provide the indispensable speed necessary to escape, but she frantically sprinted away from the predators as best she could. The barking dogs yapping in the distance were gaining, and a voice whispered, *Faster, run faster.*

Annie wrestled with her inner drive to find safety against the guilt of abandoning a friend in danger. But stopping could result in the demise of them both. Glancing back was a mistake. The toe of her boot caught on an exposed root. From nowhere, a pair of coarse and able hands grabbed her around the waist before she toppled over. The man effortlessly swept her up, placing her over his shoulder. Annie fought the urge to resist him as he carried her securely out of the forest. Her life depended on trusting he meant her no harm.

Bright sunshine obscured his face as he cautiously settled her at the base of a tree adjacent to a small church. He stepped back tentatively before walking away. Annie bent over to a kneeling position. Then crawling towards the man, her desperate voice called out to him, pleading for him to come back and hurry with her into the forest. "We have to save him," her tone was laced with fear and grief. "Please, we can't leave him there to die."

None of it was real. But that was irrelevant. Paralyzing fear and anxiety gripped Annie until a vision of Mamie Calhoun Jones emerged in the distance.

Mamie wandered in an immense field as a faint breeze stirred her billowing gray skirt. The carefree girl spread her arms wide as the sun glistened on her flawless cinnamon skin and locks of thick natural hair. With abandon, Mamie twisted and twirled in the wind. Amid a leisurely spin, her gaze settled on Annie. Angling her head to one side, Mamie's curled lips and crinkled nose were a gesture Annie recognized and cherished. The pounding terror in her chest evaporated at the familiar sight.

Mamie's outstretched arms were reminiscent of Annie's drawing after her first sighting of the striking young woman in Great Falls Village three months earlier. Annie and Mamie were now old friends if you could call it that, by way of shadowy ethereal encounters. The vision of her great-great-grandmother comforted Annie instilling calm. At long last, the thirteen-year-old drifted into a dreamless sleep.

Hours later, Annie opened her sleep-fogged eyes and lay contemplating another restless night. The reoccurring dreams of Mamie and the past were evolving. Did they hold meaning predicting the next journey to a bygone era?

Annie reached for a pencil and the sketchpad resting on the nightstand. Her hand hovered over the pad. Dismayed by an inability to capture the grim woodland scene accurately, she sketched an image of the small church. It was uncharacteristic for her to be unable to draw any picture she chose. A skilled artist, a phenom at thirteen, seasoned professionals envied the gift that flowed effortlessly from her pencil and the ability to capture most anything on paper or canvas.

Lately, Annie dedicated her artistry to creating illustrations of her ancestral family who lived long ago in Crawford, now Bibb County, Georgia. A local gallery scheduled an exhibit of the series after viewing the initial drawings. They would be stunned to learn the sketches represented a firsthand experience. Three months earlier, Annie, her sister Emma, and her cousin Joshua passed through a bewitching gateway at the Martin Luther King Jr. memorial on the mall in the nation's capital traveling back in time. It was enchanting and scary, and it changed Annie's life. Annie captured the details of the incredible adventure in a sketchbook. It documented the unusual excursion and supplied the foundation of the work she was creating for the exhibit.

But the adventure impacted more than the art. Annie acquired an obsession with the singular purpose of solving the mystery that had engrossed her family for generations. Discovering and honoring one resilient ancestor who survived the Middle Passage of the slave trade and handed that resiliency down to their descendants was the aspiration of all McElmurry and descendant time travelers. Annie was the most recent traveler, and she imagined being the one to accomplish the mission others failed to achieve.

The elders charged the wandering descendants with searching for the identity of the Unknown Ancestor. The travelers could be seeking a man or a woman, an astute youth, or a wise sage. It was an impossible charge. But trekking across history was also impossible. Yet many in her family accomplished the implausible feat of time travel. It had been passed down from one generation to another for over a hundred years, perhaps longer. It was Annie's turn now, and the name Ann Sesstry would become legendary in the McElmurry-Calhoun Clan. Mamie's recurring presence in her dreams convinced Annie she held the key to uncovering the identity of the Unknown Ancestor.

Mamie was summoning her. No sound echoed in the dreams, but Mamie's lips moved with a charm-laden expression telegraphing her purpose to her great-great-granddaughter. Mamie's spirit beckoned to her, almost daily and not merely when sleeping. Her sweet-sounding voice whispered in the warm autumn breezes. The pungent scent of Georgia's red clay somehow wafted to Annie's nose during the afternoon showers, and Mamie's laughter was caught in the plopping sounds of raindrops. Annie's senses were on alert. Her great-great-grandmother's call made all her neurons tingle. She had to heed it. There was no choice.

Her consciousness crackled in anticipation of what was to come. And this time, she would be prepared when calling upon the good people of 19th century Macon Georgia. Her research was comprehensive. The town's history, people, and geography were as well known to her as the present-day events in Fairfax County, Virginia. She was familiar with the crops grown by the local population and what food people ate. She decided it might be helpful to know the mayor, and it had not been difficult to learn his name was George Obear. Knowledge of the dreaded Black Codes, the laws designed to nullify the rights that came with emancipation, was crucial for navigating beyond the boundaries of the family. Yes, no one could be more equipped for hurling through time again than Annie.

Slipping her hand under her pillow and withdrawing the carving of the Sankofa bird, Annie propped the bird on her pillow. Her fingers raced across the page, giving flight in an artistic illustration to a bird that never flew, only moved forward in legends while gazing back.

Annie did not understand the power of the Sankofa or how the incantation of its name conjured the magic that dispatched the McElmurry descendants careening through time. Still, her instincts were firing on all cylinders, and whatever adventure awaited, this sculpture was central to what would happen again soon. Annie pressed her lips to the tiny bird's beak holding the stone. "What is your magic? Why won't you take me back when I call your name"?

Studying the sketches she'd made from her last journey for the hundredth time, Annie hoped to discover some small clue she'd missed beforehand. Annie's breath caught as she flipped to a blank page. Closing her eyes, opening them again, and blinking rapidly, Annie confirmed the blood drops falling onto the sheet of paper were real. There was blood on the statue as well. Turning her palms faced up, she gawked at her blotchy skin. Fresh blood oozed from scratches and thorn pricks covering the surface of her hands. She gazed with fascination trying to make sense of the divide between fact and fantasy as the blood and scratches slowly faded away and the page cleared.

Chapter 2

Neverland in The Mirror

Annie's alarm reverberated, interrupting her astral musings with the pulsating strain of Imani Williams' "Don't Need No Money." Annie's feet hit the floor, her head bounced, and her narrow hips swayed to the music. The up-tempo music reminded her that whatever the past held, the present required her undivided attention to gear up for school.

Sophie peeked her head into the room, checking on her daughter and offering her usual greeting. It was a gratuitous morning ritual Annie conceded to as the customary start of the day. Sophie repeated the routine with her younger daughter Emma.

"Morning, Babe."

"Morning, Mom."

Pausing before backing out, Sophie frowned.

"You should appear more refreshed just waking up in the morning. Are you dreaming of Mamie again?"

Annie impulsively massaged the smooth palm of her right hand with her left thumb.

"It will happen again soon, Mom. This time, I am ready for it."

Sophie's head throbbed with the image of Annie barreling through time but trying to make light of the situation; she tossed a glib response back to her daughter. "Just make sure it's not on a school day."

The previous spring, Annie's thirteenth birthday celebration brought the conventional rite-of-passage struggles between mothers and their teenage daughters. Now, however, Annie and Sophie's relationship was moored on a foundation rarely experienced by parents and offspring. They had grown closer after the secret chronicles of time travel by family members had been revealed and shared between them. Annie better understood her mother's drive to research the family's history. Sophie recognized Annie was sufficiently mature for bygone elders to summon her to the past. Being selected by the Unknown Ancestor and designated worthy of that invitation entitled her to more trust and independence from Sophie.

Sophie anticipated Annie illustrating their family story through her breathtaking artistic talent, as others used their unique gifts to weave a tale. But Annie was different from previous travelers as her movement through time was intimate and immersive with the ancestors. Sophie and countless other relatives had met McElmurry ancestors. But Annie's connection to their forebearers was unique; certainly, more exhaustive than the relationships Sophie or her mother Rose had forged during their travel experiences. Annie connected with the ancestors on a more personal and metaphysical level.

Annie dodged explicit questions posed by Rose and Sophie, suggesting she had not divulged the entire account of her sojourn to the past. Undoubtedly danger plagued her, Emma and Josh, and would again. Still, Sophie could not object to a future journey. The family legacy bestowed on them by the ancestors demanded trust and confidence that the Unknown would protect them in the present and the past.

"Your dad is leaving early this morning. He will drop you guys off at school. I'll pick you up this afternoon so we can go shopping for a dress for the museum opening."

Annie's hand moved unconsciously to the side of her head and scrunched her curls. "That won't work. I need to meet Kirsten after swim practice is over. Her mom will pick us up so we can work on our science assignment."

"That's not a problem. I can take you to Kirsten's house after we leave the mall."

Annie stiffened and scrunched again. "Mom, I need to go back to school. There's stuff we need to bring with us that Kirsten can't handle by herself."

Annie's deadpan expression was an attempt to appear casual and indifferent to the conversation. But her heart raced, doubtful her mother was buying her story. Sophie had a way of gingerly badgering her girls to figure out what they were up to, and Annie expected at any moment her mother would start the squeeze to learn why returning to school after their shopping trip concluded was so important.

Annie's flush and the tell-tale hair scrunching betrayed her, telegraphing to her mother that this supposed academic excursion had nothing at all to do with science. Surprisingly, Sophie let it pass. Okay then, I'll take you back to school, and Dad can pick you up from Kirsten's on his way home from work. He'll probably be working late, with the opening this weekend, so Kirsten's mom needs to include you in dinner."

Sophie shut the door, and Annie danced across the floor, straight into her bathroom. Jay Anders was Annie's first serious crush. Tall with swagger and a killer smile, she closed her eyes and pictured him moving down the hall, backpack slung across his shoulder, grabbing the attention of half the girls at school. He was on the swim team with her best friend, Kirsten. Without a doubt, Jay was the epitome of cool. Pouting and primping moony-eyed into the mirror, she practiced a range of expressions she would use when she not so randomly bumped into him later that day.

On a few occasions, Jay had been checking her out. She wasn't so naïve that she didn't recognize when a boy scrutinized her with interest. Today, if her strategy succeeded, they would have an extended conversation. The original plan was to wait for Kirsten in the pool bleachers. She would do her homework feigning indifference to him, though he would spot her. Waiting by the lockers for Kirsten when Jay came out, he would strike up a conversation. It would be up to her to break the ice if he didn't. "Hi Jay," she purred into the mirror.

That plan was now out. Meeting Kirsten after practice would have to do. A text to Kirsten making her aware Annie was outside to steer Jay in her direction had to be timed perfectly. Before Kirsten's mom arrived, they could still have a conversation, and he could be her date for the fall dance. At least in theory, since her parents would not agree to an actual date at thirteen. But her presence side by side with Jay in the gym would make it evident to everyone that they were together.

Anne showered, and withdrawing from the bathroom, found Emma in her room, dancing.

"Why are you in here?" taunted Annie.

"For the music, of course. This song is one of my favorites, and it beckoned to me as I passed by your door. Do you think there will be music at the museum opening?"

"Beckoned you, huh. Who are you? And no, there will not be music for dancing, now remove yourself from my room, snapped Annie."

"Why," cooed Emma, "so you can primp for Jay Anders?"

"I am warning you, Emma, stop eavesdropping on my conversations."

Emma puckered her lips, making kissing sounds, and wiggled to the beat. Grabbing a pillow from the bed and tossing it at Emma, Annie shouted, "Out!"

Emma shimmied out as Annie watched her sister with begrudging affection. She had grown more magnanimous towards Emma since their unexpected visit to nineteenth-century Crawford County, Georgia. Inexplicably, being whisked through a portal taking them to another century had been forgotten by Emma and Josh. Annie surmised it was because they had not reached their thirteenth birthdays. All the McElmurry travelers hopped through time following their thirteenth birthdays. Fox assumed Emma and Josh were pulled into the travel vortex by mistake. Their grandmother Rose insisted the Ancestors did not make mistakes. Eventually, the Ancestors would reveal the reason for Josh and Emma's visit to the past.

Time travel had been a life-altering experience for Annie, but not for Emma and Josh since they could not recollect the whirlwind rush through time, a shift to the past on a blistering summer day without a breeze to offer relief from the heat. July 23, 1867, Fox McElmurry, a renaissance man of the past, registered to vote for the first time on that day. As for his three precocious descendants from the future, well, the day was just as memorable for them as it was for Fox.

In the span of a few hours, Annie, Josh, and Emma leaned and lived a history lesson never taught in school. They discovered Black life in Georgia during Reconstruction. Surprisingly, family get-to-gethers one hundred and fifty years ago turned out to be not so different than a family gathering in Virginia today. They were humbled by how much their ancestors had to overcome for them to have the lives they now enjoyed. The three met folk who, until that day, had been random names on the family tree.

Stirred by the ancestor whose name she bore and the other Ann's desperation to learn to read, Annie gained a new appreciation for her education. Over a short period, she matured as few teens ever would. It was not difficult to vividly recall that sticky summer afternoon. Sweat trickled down her arms in the unforgiving heat, and mosquitos located every exposed spot on her legs to suckle, but she would not trade that day for anything.

Her heart held the blissful sound of laughter and the pungent scent of honeysuckle in the air. The three lunched in a picnic grove over a hundred and fifty years ago in a forgotten era. She captured the fantastic voyage in one of her ever-present sketchbooks and listened to stories told by Fox. It would have been perfect was it not for the kidnapping of Emma and their ancestor, Mary Jane McElmurry.

Annie shuddered as she recalled the harrowing nightmare of Emma's kidnapping, putting her in danger of being sold the way many other Black orphans were after the Civil War. Maybe it was best Emma couldn't recall being taken and nearly bartered away for money or anything else needed in the distressed South of 1867. Annie's fear of losing Emma was dreadful. She never wanted to endure anything so frightening again. It was the one event of their travels omitted whenever Annie retold her implausible tale. She believed Emma would eventually remember, and it would be her story to share.

Shifting her attention to the mirror to finish dressing, Annie was startled by the images before her. She was no longer viewing herself in the mirror; she was gazing at a reflection of another time in their family history. The scene before her was an elaborate celebration. People wearing elegant clothing from another vintage age were smiling and socializing. Annie did not immediately recognize any people until she saw Mamie among the guests. She was older than the girl Annie first met. She possessed the same sweet expression, and though Annie sensed something different about her, there was no doubt it was Mamie.

Examining the scene with an artist's eye for detail, Annie recognized the man and woman at the center of attention. In a family photo collage, her grandmother Rose kept a picture of her great-grandparents, Joshua and Missouri Calhoun. This fanciful celebration was the observation of their fiftieth wedding anniversary. Tastefully dressed in a gray silk belted suit with a jeweled buckle and white blouse, Missouri inspected her surroundings, ensuring everything was perfect. She wore laced shoes with a small heel. Pearls draped her long neck, and her hair was parted down the middle and pulled back.

Joshua had a stern but proud expression. He sported a patterned silk vest and matching tie that accented his distinguished suit. A gold chain was visible from the bottom of his vest. Annie observed as he withdrew a gold pocket watch from the end of the chain and checked the hour. All around, the guests elbowed to reach Mr. and Mrs. Calhoun to offer congratulations. The Calhoun family and friends filled a table with the dozens of presents commemorating the occasion. Expensive household gifts exemplary of such a special occasion would one day become family heirlooms. The food table was set with stunningly fine crystal and china and spread with sumptuous food, assorted pastries, fruits, vegetables, and meats. To her amazement, Annie could smell the delicious offerings.

Joshua Calhoun pranced around the spacious parlor accepting well wishes with the hubris of a peacock. Displaying a gracious and classy demeanor, Missouri warmly greeted their guests.

Annie glanced at Mamie, who was standing beside a small-framed man. Annie recognized Mamie's husband, her great-great-grandfather, Ransom Jones. Mamie's eyebrows bobbed up as she acknowledged Annie. She pressed two fingers to her lips, blowing a kiss to her great-great-granddaughter across the ages.

Riveted by the scene in the mirror, Annie blinked rapidly as the picture faded and was replaced by another. Youngsters spanning multiple ages played in the yard of the sprawling plantation-style home. Thick white stately columns adorned a massive porch wrapped around the house. A couple sat in a mammoth swing swaying gently back and forth, watching the children. The young guests wore their Sunday best, matching the adults inside the house.

As Annie studied the picture before her, she gasped as her eyes settled on two of the children. Emma and Josh were playing with the others comfortable in their surroundings. They were not images or likenesses of long-gone ancestors; it was them. Someone else was standing observing Josh and Emma. He was tall and slim, but the position of his body obscured his face; still, she mused, there was something familiar about him. It couldn't be someone from the first visit, given many years had passed.

Recalling her family history Annie realized this was Lizella Georgia, on the outskirts of Macon, and it was February 3, 1935. But what were Emma and Josh doing there? Her eyes fixated on the door of the elegant home. Mamie stood intently studying Annie with her head tilted and the familiar outstretched hands. Staring at Mamie's extended arms, a sudden assurance struck Annie. *She's signaling to me. We're not returning to 1867; we're going to another era.*

"We're traveling to a different century to experience a different chapter in our family's Neverland story," she whispered as the image faded.

Chapter 3

Tracing the Road Back

*T*he tribal lands of the Muskogee Indians swirled at the water's edge of the Ocmulgee River in Macon, Georgia. The indigenous people of central Georgia were called Creek. Distinguished for their prowess as hunters and fierce protectors of their families, the Creek guardedly coexisted with the colonizers of the state named in honor of King George II. The neutral accord between the Indians and the settlers lasted until the rise of a different king. The lucrative crop of king cotton and the spread of the depraved practice of slavery foreshadowed doom for the Creek.

The United States Government brutalized the tribes, confiscated the territory, and forced the true heirs from their land. The Creek Nation slogged the Trail of Tears with other native people from Florida, Alabama, and North Carolina. Wrenched from their ancestral homeland, they advanced to the Western front. The Government drove over one hundred thousand people from the territory. They were Cherokee, Chickasaw, Choctaw, and Seminole. Legend maintains that the Creeks cursed the countryside as they left, declaring the settlers would never leave the poached territory. But the consequences of a curse are seldom confined to its original intentions.

At the beginning of the 19th century, enslaved men, women, and children constituted roughly half of Georgia's population. The Creek curse *afflicted those held in bondage and toiling the soil as much if not more than the settlers who claimed the land as their own. The affliction was more debilitating to the persecuted laborers than those who plundered the land. The enslaved were bound to the farmland by subjugation, not by choice. Chained to the earth cursed by the Creeks, the grind and sweat of these people formed the bedrock of Southern prosperity. Their captors would go to any lengths to control their prisoners and keep them shackled to the farmstead. The wealth of the Georgia plantation class grew with the expansion of free labor. Slavers and the oppressed, both yoked to the same land but in incongruent ways.*

In 1825 on a Macon plantation owned by Levi Calhoun, an enslaved girl gave birth in a dilapidated cabin on a dirt-packed floor. The healthy baby boy was given the name Noah. The family history notes that Noah's mother was born in Virginia and sold to an enslaver in Georgia. No additional information is available on her Virginia family members. The history of the first Georgians is in the old Virginia historical records; thus, the Virginia - Georgia slave exchange was predictable and commonplace.

Seven years after Noah's birth, a midwife delivered a baby girl named Sophia on that same estate. Census records did not include slave births; thus, no records from that period mention Sophia or Noah's parents. Noah and Sophia experienced the early years of life in shabby pine-board cabins unfit for human habitation. Slave quarters lacked durable windows and doors, and the winter winds tore through the structures as families hovered under tattered blankets fighting to keep the elements at bay. In the summer, the sweltering heat and swarming mosquitos made it nearly impossible to sleep, though the inhabitants were allotted very few hours for the luxury of rest.

The chattel workers labored in the fields and the home serving those profanely dubbed masters. As time passed, Noah and Sophia joined to become a family. Their flock was perpetually at risk and vulnerable to an ideology that held no respect towards the Black family unit. The dismal lives of the enslaved were predictable yet imperiled by the whims and economic fortunes of the enslaver. Sophia and Noah lived in fear of losing a child to the auction block.

The hub of the Calhoun Plantation was an imposing antebellum mansion. The pillared French colonial exterior included a wide wrap-around porch shaded by a second-story veranda. Levi could stand on the veranda and survey his assets, including men, women, and children he deemed undeserving of freedom. Orval Calhoun Sr. was born in that house. As the eldest son of Levi, he was confident, privileged, and unrestrained by the precepts of the law.

Presumably, Orval was unaware of the Creek curse. Position and inheritance indentured Orval to the family estate and obliged him to preserve the way of life to which he, Noah, and Sophia had been born. When the drums of war called, the sons of Georgia answered. Orval fought for the South in the Confederate Army to protect everything he cherished; all he'd been raised to believe he was entitled to, including ownership of mortal men and women. At the end of the war, he returned home defeated with the meaningless military rank of Captain.

The law required Orval to sign the Oath of Allegiance, a loyalty pledge to the Constitution of the United States of America. The promise was a prerequisite for him to retain ownership of his property. Orval did not survive the post-war afflictions, the price he was to pay for his plantation, and the South to be restored to greatness as he imagined they would be. Life and war took their toll, and he died in 1868 at the age of thirty-eight. His wife Eliza governed what was left of the Calhoun Plantation until her sons came of age.

The two eldest sons, Orval Jr. and Edward assumed control of the family land and the custody of the sharecroppers who harvested the fields. Sharecroppers were the tenant farmers who planted, tilled, and plowed a small plot of land in exchange for housing, farming resources, and a portion of the crops when the harvest concluded. In truth, it was little more than debt-slavery since the sharecroppers owed the landowners usury sums of money for provisions, farm tools, and rent. They had little hope of climbing out of the cycle of debt and poverty, and almost all died in nothing more than a synthetic form of freedom.

Noah and Sophia's son Joshua was among the exceptions. Joshua took as his wife Missouri, the daughter of Fox and Mary McElmurry. Missouri understood the significance of acquiring property and the value of an education. Lacking a formal education himself, Joshua relied on

Missouri to serve as wife and teacher. He abided by her request that their children be educated. Joshua Calvin Calhoun became a prominent landholder and businessman in Macon, Georgia, and with his wife, Missouri, transformed the generations that followed.

Chapter 4

The Museum

Irritated, Annie moped around her bedroom. She listlessly dressed for the first event marking the grand opening of the African American Museum of History and Culture. Her miserable frame of mind stemmed from her failed plan to ambush Jay Anders after swim practice on Thursday. Despite all the contrivance, Annie did not *accidentally* bump into Jay. Jay was excused from practice to attend a family function to her dismay and disappointment.

Who cares why he wasn't there? Whatever the reason, her plans ran aground. Undeterred, she attempted throughout the day to run into him at school on Friday. She'd taken different routes to her classes. But she wasn't familiar with his schedule, and he could have been anywhere in the school. They didn't have the same lunch period, where in-school social mingling occurred. All her efforts proved fruitless. This was no different from the swim practice fiasco. No sightings of Jay Anders. Giving up on randomly bumping into him had been her last best hope. She now wondered if her intention of making them an item before the fall dance had any chance of succeeding.

As she slipped on the navy-blue dress she and her mother picked out, she sighed. If she didn't land on Jay's radar soon, the fall dance would fizzle. She probably wouldn't bother attending. There would be no point. Every girl there would be jockeying for his attention.

She examined her reflection in the mirror and wished Jay could feast his eyes on her tonight. She had to admit to herself; she looked hot. This dress was sophisticated and more grown-up than anything in her closet.

The dress was sleeveless with a v-neckline, and a dropped wasted that emphasized her maturing figure. She wore the locket her grandparents had given her last Christmas and pearl earrings with a matching bracelet. Sheer pantyhose and low navy pumps completed her outfit. Her mother had flat-ironed her hair. It had been a while since she had worn it straight, and tonight it shinned and streamed down her back. Tonight, Annie mused, she could grace the cover of Teen Vogue. *Too bad it's wasted on a bunch of adults.*

Putting aside her disappointment, Annie focused on the weekend's celebrations. Famous individuals from all over would be there. Athletes, television and movie stars, and influential people worldwide contributed to the museum's construction. Equally impressive was that everyday people discovered they possessed valuable artifacts significant to Black History. By donating their possessions to the museum, they guaranteed the preservation of their heritage in perpetuity. Thousands would attend the celebrations at the museum and parties all over the city.

The museum's grand opening was the culmination of years of hard work, and the city was in a celebratory mood. Tonight's reception was for donors. Tomorrow's official ceremony would include President and Mrs. Obama and former President and Mrs. Bush. President George W. Bush had authorized the legislation to build the museum on federal land in 2003. *That was the same year I was born.* Annie appreciated the significance of the effort invested in this weekend and the assembly of the museum and its contents.

The Sesstry family was fortunate. John's position with the Smithsonian assured his family's presence at all the main events. This evening, Annie, Emma, and Josh would attend the pre-opening tour and reception and tomorrow's grand opening and dedication. Her parents, grandparents, and aunt would attend the twilight black-tie gala. The kids would not be present at the gala, but their celebration would continue. A suite was booked at a hotel downtown for Annie,

Emma, and Josh to stay for the evening. Each could invite a friend over for pizza and movies until their parents returned.

Satisfied with her appearance, Annie drifted into Emma's room. "Awesome hookup, Emms."

"Seriously? Everything matches. Not my style. And my hair is straight out of another decade. Who wears their hair straight anymore? Curls are in, and mine are the bomb."

Emma wore a full-skirted floral dress with a pink sash. Across the top of her head was a fitted headband matching her outfit. Pink tights and black ballet flats rounded out the ensemble.

"How on earth did Mom come up with this getup? The one for tomorrow is worse. She has me channeling Sasha Obama."

"Doesn't matter how much you complain; you're still gorgeous. And chill out. The opening of the museum is insanely significant, especially to Dad. Mom wanted us to step up our game for his sake. Tonight, and tomorrow we're Dad's daughters. Monday, we go back to being us. I'm going to present as the perfect daughter and tolerate being Ann since Mom is sure to call me that all weekend and you will be the younger princess in waiting."

The girls trounced down their Great Falls home's back staircase to join their mother. Sophie was in the kitchen wearing a stunning green silk suit stood Sophie. She beamed with satisfaction as she gazed at her daughters. "You girls are absolutely stunning."

"Who's that?" mocked Emma, tossing her head towards her mother.

"You've got me. I think it's someone impersonating our mother."

"Very funny," countered Sophie. "It's not as if it's the first time I've ever been dressed up."

"It's fancy and a lot more conservative than anything you wear for book signings and stuff," said Emma. "And what's with the makeup? Who did that to your face?"

"Stop. I had it done at the mall, and the style is right for the occasion."

"So, who are you tonight, Sophia or Sophie?" Annie smirked at the duplicity of her mother going by a derivative of her given name while insisting on referring to her daughter as Ann, not her preferred Annie.

Sashaying across the kitchen towards the door leading to the garage, Sophie affected an exaggerated southern accent. "Why, I am Mrs. Sophia Clarkson Sesstry of Virginia, accompanied by my daughters, Misses Ann and Emma Sesstry. We are attending one of the most meaningful events of the century; the constructed testimonial of the contributions of the African American to the abundance of these United States."

Annie sneered as the three headed out of the door.

On the drive to the museum, Sophie stopped to pick up her sister Lizzy Cooper and nephew Josh. Lizzy wore a striking purple suit with a pencil skirt, long sleeves, and a wraparound gold belt. Black pumps with gold heels capped her outfit. Contrary to most boys his age, Josh was comfortable dressed up. He sported a navy blazer, red and navy striped tie, and khaki pants. His Harry Potter glasses sat perfectly on solid nose. The family's buoyant temperament and festive attire were compatible with the excitement of the evening.

Traffic was thick as they neared the National Mall, requiring Sophie to park blocks away from the museum. The brisk hike to the three-tiered structure among dozens of other guests headed in that direction added to the vibrancy of the evening. Once they arrived, the dazzling bronze facade greeted them, and the exhilarating atmosphere enveloped the crowd of visitors. The animated buzz was contagious as they proceeded to the entrance of the building that resembled an inverted pyramid.

The residents of the DMV, the standard byname for the Washington Metropolitan area, had witnessed over the last several years the construction of the towering building along Constitution Avenue that would house the artifacts of Black America. Still, nothing prepared the Sesstry and Cooper families for the completed structure that inspired them when they stepped through the entrance. It was a historic occasion for sure. Black people assuming their place in the nation's capital, and the country finally affirming their contributions and rightful narrative. The rich history of the people of

African descent in America was at last fully legitimized. Uniformed guides greeted guests, handing out maps of the museum and programs for the night's events. The animated party spotted Rose and Byron Clarkson across the gleaming lobby by the information desk. Annie, Emma, and Josh rushed to greet their grandparents.

"John is bursting." Rose chuckled. "You'd think he built the museum with his own two hands. He said we should start exploring, and he would catch up with us later."

"Where should we start?" asked Lizzy.

"The underground exhibits mark the beginning of the slave trade and our people's history in America. That's the place to begin," answered Sophie.

The group boarded the elevator leading to the lower gallery. Sophie mentioned an article she'd read about the plans for the museum with a precise vision in mind for the elevators. The mesmerizing experience of descending to the sub-basement level would simulate a journey back in time.

The designers etched dates on the shaft walls delineating the milestones of the African American experience. As the melodic and eloquent tone of the elevator operator's voice took the passengers from the twenty-first to the seventeenth century, the spirituality and call of the ancestors drew them closer to their heritage. The car arrived at its destination, and the faintest sounds of drums filtered through the structure.

A different vibe accosted the family as they exited the elevator at the lower galleries. If the intent was to strike a contrast from the contemporary entrance to this muted memorial to the beginning of the African's experience in a new country, they nailed it, mulled Annie. The main level flaunted shiny floors and highlighted testimonials to major donors. This level was contrary. The ceilings here were subjacent, with narrow passages by traditional museum standards. Visitors could effortlessly examine displays under the bright lights installed for reading the title cards and exhibit commentary. But the surrounding lights were restrained and shadowy.

Sophie inhaled, preparing for a glance back in time. The Sesstry clan made their way along the corridors, intently examining the exhibits. The displays were a chronology of the transatlantic slave trade and the Middle Passage. This triangular route took ships from Europe to Africa. They bartered goods for kidnapped Africans before continuing to the Atlantic coast to sell their human cargo before returning to Europe.

Sophie and Lizzy alternated in pointing out unusual artifacts and exhibitions to the youngsters. The family moved from one display to another, examining individual collections and absorbing the history of their ancestors and the descendants of Africa. Josh bristled at the sight of shackles that once circled the arms and legs of captured Africans. Even secure in the awareness that four hundred years had passed to witness the vulnerability of their ancestors was sobering. Here was the evidence of the cruelty and subjugation pressed upon their forebears. A humble reverence pierced the atmosphere of the integrated span of rooms as spectators spoke in hushed tones.

Cryptic sensations saturated Annie's slender body, causing the tiny hairs on her arms to stand up. The temperature around her dropped, and instantly, she was in the presence of the spirits of the Unknown Ancestors. As the atmosphere changed, a chilled breath passed along the back of her neck. A fierce haze of emotion engulfed Annie, and her head began to spin. The grief-stricken wails of mothers and lost children pounded in her chest. The shouts of men captured and chained grew in intensity. The sounds were deafening.

Annie scrambled from the glass display, putting distance between her and her family. Taking deep breaths, she struggled to regain control. With no destination in mind, she found herself at the exhibit illustrating the transportation of captive Africans on slave ships. It held portions of the Portuguese ship *São José Paquete Africa*. The boat sank off the coast of South Africa in 1794, with four hundred kidnapped Africans confined below deck.

She reminisced on Fox and his time travel to a slave ship and the long search for the family he'd never met, names lost in history. His ancestor survived the fate of a boat similar to this one, only to weather the voyage and land in unfamiliar, hostile territory at the mercy of enslavers. Gazing at the illustrations of the mournful human cargo laid out side by side, heartache engulfed her, and a single tear slid down her cheek.

"It's hard to believe it happened, isn't it?"

Annie quickly swiped her face and swiveled around to determine who'd been rude enough to intrude upon her private reflections. Her knees locked, shocked by the sight of the object of her waking fantasies for the last several weeks. In front of her, confident and handsome in a suit and tie stood Jay Anders.

Before she could consider an appropriate response, the words blurted out, "What are you doing here?"

A cocky expression of amusement spread across his face as Jay pointed to a woman leading a group through the museum. "My Aunt Lisa's firm built the museum. She works for McKissick and McKissick. She was the program director for this project. And the senior program manager for the Martin Luther King Memorial too."

Try as she might, Annie could think of nothing intelligent to say. "You missed swim practice yesterday."

"Yeah, there was a museum celebration at my aunt's firm, and she wanted the whole family there."

Jay's wilily expression of satisfaction confirmed Annie's worse fears.

She wanted to sink through the floor. *Why should I know he missed swim practice? Oh God, he thinks I'm interested in him or that I'm a stalker. But I am interested in him.* She groaned inwardly.

Saved by the approach of her father, she'd never been so happy to have him insinuate himself into one of her conversations. She even welcomed his peck on the cheek. *Here comes some corny comment.*

"Hi, baby." Directing his attention to the young man talking to his daughter, he added, "How are you tonight, Jay?"

"Fine, thanks, Mr. Sesstry."

"You know him?" stuttered Annie.

"Sure, his aunt, Lisa Anders, was lead on the museum project. She's a fellow Howard Bison. She went to the School of Engineering, then on to the University of Maryland for graduate school. How are you two familiar with each other?"

"Jay and I go to the same school."

"Small world," exclaimed John cluelessly, strolling towards the rest of the family. An awkward silence settled between Annie and Jay as they stood sizing one another up. Jay switched his weight from one foot to the other. Annie fiddled with her locket. She caught a glimpse of her mother monitoring her with the realization her mother was aware all along the science project was a ruse. Sophie took her finger and pulled up the side of her mouth, gesturing for Annie to smile. Then she motioned for her daughter to take her hand from the necklace and toss her hair.

Annie suppressed a giggle.

She's giving me flirting lessons here of all places. And throw my hair? She would never do that, in fact, who does that besides airheads with nothing to say?

Ignoring her mother, Annie focused on Jay. "You must be very familiar with the museum,", elated to be talking to him at last. *Who could have imagined the day would end up better than I could have imagined.*

"Yeah, that's all anyone in my family has talked about for months, years, I should say. How much of it have you explored so far?"

"Not a lot; we've barely started."

"I can show you the highlights on this one and floor above. There's no way you can probe the whole place in a few hours. It will take several visits to check out everything. There is so much to survey. After that you will want to come back every so often as they change out the exhibits. But I'm sure your dad will keep you up to date on new displays. I will probably have to check with you since my aunt's work is done here."

There it was again. *That smile, that cocky, killer smile.*

The two young people settled into a comfortable rhythm as they completed the lower concourse and moved up to the next level to the Defending Freedom, Defining Freedom Exhibit. The early years of African American freedom, Jim Crow, and the Civil Rights Movement were the level's central theme. Annie was impressed by the extent of Jay's knowledge, but she could hold her own. She had, after all, grown up in a family dedicated to telling the story of their ancestors and African people brought to America in slavery.

As they approached the somber exhibit of Emmett Till's casket, they passed a replica of an outdated cabin. The title card read The Freedom House. The front displayed a bronze sculpture of a woman sitting in a rocking chair. Jay's words faded into obscurity as the statue of the woman transformed into a living being. Pitching back and forth in the chair was Missouri McElmurry Calhoun.

Annie inhaled loudly enough for Jay to hear.

Jay eyeballed her quizzically, and then studied the sculpture. "If I had not been present at the installation of this exhibit and admired the architect's workmanship, I would swear that chair moved."

"That's ludicrous," proclaimed Annie, "the bolts holding it down are visible.

Grabbing Jay's hand, she maneuvered him away from the cabin, gazing back one last time, she again observed a living Missouri. This time Mamie was standing beside her with the all too familiar tilt of her head.

Signaling, Annie shook her head and pleaded with her eyes. *Not now, please, not now.*

Chapter 5

The Great Camp Meeting in The Promised Land

Noah Calhoun and Fox McElmurry shared a vision and a mutual determination to rise above the station of sharecroppers. Both men had large families. Fox and his wife Mary had ten children, Ann, William, Cicero, Mary Jane, Amos, Missouri, Francis, Johnny, and Emma. Noah and Sophia had eight, Abraham, Noah Jr, Joshua, Narcissa, Georgiana, Thelma, Thomas, and Frances.

Large families meant extra workers and increased profitability sharecropping. The higher profits generated by more workers increased the possibility of land ownership. Fox acquired his first parcel of land in 1880. It took Noah more or less the same amount of time to own property after working for others. Both men were religious and sustained by faith. The Calhoun and McElmurry families were frequent attendees at the traveling religious revivals making their way across the South, as were many Black families pursuing spiritual fulfillment.

Camp meetings, the term used for the revivals, took on a holiday atmosphere. Raucous festive affairs were customary, along with music, singing, and preaching; lots of preaching demanding devotees repent. One might question why formerly enslaved congregants needed repentance after their miseries. Still, in need or not,, many, including Noah, Fox, and their respective families, attended as many revivals as possible.

These religious events were a bedrock of Black life in the South after the Civil War and continued throughout the Jim Crow era. They often went on for five days, providing a chance for people to congregate, meet, and socialize. The worshippers released their anxieties and fears through praise and prayer. They murmured amens, did the Holy Ghost dance, and shouted hallelujahs. People shed pent-up tears and let down their hair. The revivals were social events where people found compatible friends and even life partners. At one such gathering, Joshua Calhoun and Missouri McElmurry began their courtship.

"That boy's got his eye on you," teased Mary Jane McElmurry to her younger sister, Missouri.

"I ain't studin' Joshua Calhoun."

"Well, for someone not interested, his name rolled off your tongue mighty easy."

Both girls collapsed in a fit of giggles. Missouri dared to steal a glimpse of Joshua, who chose to take a full appraisal of her at the exact moment. Embarrassed to have been caught peeking, Missouri pretended to lose herself in the hymn, "There's a Great Camp Meeting in the Promised Land." She raised her hands in devoted praise and swayed to the music with her eyes closed.

"I sense a little more than the Holy Ghost got you, child," came her mother Mary's voice from behind her.

Missouri glanced back, blushing at her mother's words.

"Mr. Noah Calhoun spoke to your papa bout young Joshua there comin' round to keep company."

"What does Papa think?"

"Fox says that boy ain't got much, sides a cow, a mule, and a slew of ambition. I think that might be enough. What do you think?"

"Brother declares he can't even read," whispered Mary Jane as Preacher Turner started his sermon.

"Most colored folks can't read." Missouri hissed.

Fox's icy gaze communicated to his daughters that it was time to be quiet and pay attention to the message.

Henry McNeal Turner was the most famous Macon preacher of his generation. He was born free in South Carolina in 1834. He was an African Methodist Episcopal minister, and people came from far and wide to listen to his sermons. Turner was well-traveled. He could read and write, and he was the first Black chaplain for Colored Troops in the United States Army. He served during the Civil War, and following his military service, he was appointed to the Freedmen's Bureau in Georgia and settled in Macon.

His stature brought demands on his time, and it was a rare treat for him to be home and available to preach at a local revival. He would one day become the Chancellor of Morris Brown College, where Mamie, the oldest child of Joshua and Missouri Calhoun, would attend.

It was a steamy summer day, and Pastor Turner deviated from the variation of sermons usually preached at camp meetings. His words were at odds with the typical fire and brimstone exhortations to pray and repent. He did not evangelize about redemption and salvation.

His words today were utterances of anger and bitterness against the United States and, more specifically, against the state of Georgia. Turner harbored resentment at being denied his seat in the Georgia State Senate; the citizens of his district had duly elected him to the position. The words of his "I Claim the Rights of a Man" speech spread throughout colored society after white elected officials expelled him and twenty-six other Black representatives from the state legislature. On this day, Turner's defiance toward the system was on full display.

"There is no instance mentioned in history where an enslaved people of an alien race rose to respectability upon the same territory of their enslavement and in the presence of their enslavers, without losing their identity or individuality by amalgamation. Our ancestors surrendered their identities and individuality, but I say to you no more. Brothers and sisters, we must reclaim our identities. We must teach our children who they are while the alien race attempts to destroy those identities and gives nothing in exchange."

"I know we are Americans to all intents and purposes. We are born here, raised here, fought, bled, and died here and have a thousand times more right here than hundreds of thousands of those who help to snub, proscribe, and persecute us, and that is one of the reasons I almost despise the land of my birth. Almost, but not quite. I cannot fully despise a place where a mighty God granted me the blessings of family and friends; a land where I was could serve in the Army, minister to colored soldiers, and play a role in unbinding my race. Against all odds, I was born free and lived to see my people released from bondage. It is a country with potential; yes, it is a land of opportunity even for us gathered here today. Here I stand before you, pleading with you, begging you to seize the moment and to make this country a better place until the day comes when we can return to our fatherland."

When Turner finished his sermon, there were no customary amens or hallelujahs. Instead, a hushed silence lingered among the worshipers as they made their way out of the sanctuary. There was a relentless admission of what was and speculation of what should and could be.

With the first service of the day concluded, Missouri and Mary Jane strolled around the enormous tent greeting neighbors and friends, picking up murmurs regarding Pastor Turner's message., Missouri observed most were not sure what to make of it. It was contrary to the revival sermons local preachers typically delivered. Trials, tribulations, and Lord have mercy.

She and Mary Jane talked between themselves about the unusual message as they made their way outside the temporary sanctuary to the food stations set up in an open field. Tables filled with lunch dishes, baked goods, and beverages were abundant. As the day progressed, the variety and number of food choices would increase. The two young women approached the lemonade site as Joshua Calhoun fell in stride with Missouri.

Mary, who was serving along with other women, motioned for Mary Jane to give her sister and Joshua time to become better acquainted.

"Good day, Missouri."

Missouri was tall for a girl, but since Joshua was over six feet tall, she had to crane her neck to peer up at him.

"Good day, Joshua."

"You are exceedingly striking today." Joshua pronounced. That is a lovely dress you're wearing. Blue suits you.

"Thank you very much." Missouri flushed.

Joshua extended his arm for Missouri, who hesitated for only a moment before tucking her arm through his. She drew a fan from her pocket and gently waved it back and forth as they strolled away from the crowd along a path.

"What did you think of Pastor Turner's sermon this morning?"

Missouri paused. "Well, I was surprised a preacher would lament the circumstances of colored folks and, for once, not let God off the hook for the unfairness of it all. Most of these preachers tell us to trust God, to be patient and wait for redemption and a heavenly reward once we're dead."

"So, you believe God has been unfair to colored people?"

The question confounded Missouri. "Don't you?"

Joshua stopped walking adjusting his stance to look Missouri in the eye.

"Folks have been mistreated throughout time, Missouri. The Israelites suffered countless years under the Egyptians. The Good Book says four hundred. I believe God set the world to spinning and let man have at it. He ain't the cause of man's sins and problems, and he ain't gonna be the answer either."

At that moment Missouri developed a deeper insight into Joshua, thinking his words corresponded to her father's.

"If God ain't gonna fix it, then who is and what is the answer?" she challenged.

"Weren't you listening to Pastor Turner? We got to fix it, and before we can improve on the world's problems, we got to set our situation right and stop thinking the white man is ever gonna care whether we make it or not. We all got to make our own way. I, for one, am gonna make a fine way for my family."

"Do tell. And how are you going to go about doing that?"

A formidable scowl covered Joshua's face. Glancing around at the open fields, he declared, "I will be the most successful Negro farmer in these parts. I will own more land in this county than any other Negro man around and more than many white folks too. With property comes power and respect, and I intend to have both."

Missouri shot Joshua a withering gaze.

"Well, I hope you have a strong wife to help you. My papa says women are as smart and necessary to a man's success as anything else. And I believe he's right."

With that, Missouri spun on her heels and walked back to the sanctuary tent.

Joshua broke out into a rare, full-fledged grin.

Thus began the courtship of Joshua Calhoun and Missouri McElmurry. On February 3, 1885, they were married. It was a union of mutual respect and common pursuits that would last nearly fifty-one years. Missouri came with a dowry gifted by Fox to his daughter and new son-in-law. He gave them fifty acres of prime McElmurry land.

Chapter 6

Back to Neverland

Annie never paid much attention to the adventures of Peter Pan and the Lost Boys detailed in the play by James Barrie until her encounter with Mamie in 1912. Her great-great-grandmother was reading the book when they met and told her young visitors that she planned to use the story with her students when she became a teacher. After the encounter with Mamie, the book became a symbol to Annie of the McElmurry's time travels. It also represented the plight of Africans, taken from their homeland and brought to America against their will.

The boys of Neverland were orphans, lost to their families forever; her kidnapped ancestors were waifs as well. They had vanished precipitously from their homeland. To their families, they, like the lost boys, were irrevocably gone without a trace from those who loved them. In both Barrie's tale and in the horrors of the slave trade, innocents disappeared when someone failed to comprehend the evil dangers of ships and anonymous abductors. An accurate depiction of Neverland confirms it was not a magical or happy place. It was fraught with risks, and its inhabitants struggled for survival one day at a time. Such was the case in America for the enslaved.

The more Annie explored the history of her ancestors, the more she understood the hazards of their struggles to survive in a system stacked against them. Her school lessons taught little regarding the tribulations of slavery. A few teachers even tried to recast what happened during slavery as little more than indentured servitude. But historians such as her mother were dedicated to exposing the truth. The Unknown Ancestors used the miracle of time travel to launch their descendants to significant periods of their history, enabling them to witness the era's reality and then recount the story in their own words.

Since the odd apparitions in the mirror the day before, Annie understood Neverland was not a destination but an abstraction characterizing the life experiences of her ancestors. The Unknown would catapult them to someplace in or around Macon, Georgia, at some far-off time. Wherever and whenever they happened to place the voyagers would be their next Neverland adventure. Each brush with her forebearers was another intricate piece of an elaborate puzzle, a new lesson in the family history. It would be irony to travel to bygone times on the day of the official opening of the African American History Museum.

Annie readied herself for the day's celebrations, mindful that the festivities at the museum would be secondary to whatever else occurred. Confident she, Emma, and Josh would travel through time today, her anticipation escalated. The previous day's developments persuaded her they would not be going back to 1912 or 1867 but to 1935 to commemorate the fiftieth wedding anniversary of Missouri and Joshua Calhoun. She was under no illusion the purpose of traveling to the anniversary party would be to allow them solely to participate in the celebration. Nothing about journeying through time was that simple. She had to stay alert to avert a major crisis resembling their initial time hop.

Still, the idea of skipping almost seventy years between visits was unsettling. Annie didn't understand how she would unlock the past by jumping across decades. She needed consistent and sequential information to solve the mystery of the Unknown Ancestor. The further she moved away from the day of the Unknown's arrival in America, the less plausible it would be to meet people who could help in the blanks of her family history.

"Naturally, this would have to be today," she mumbled. "I've spent the past three weeks maneuvering for Jay Anders's attention, and now that I have it, I must excuse myself to take a voyage through yesteryear. What do I say if he approaches me at the museum again? "I would love to talk and continue our tour, but I have an appointment in 1935 with my great-great-great-grandmother, Missouri McElmurry Calhoun. You failed to see her rocking in the chair in front of the Freedom Cabin last night."

Emma shoved open the door, strolling into Annie's room.

"Are you talking to yourself again?"

"Emma, when are you going to learn to knock?"

"Where would the fun be in that?"

Anxiously moving things around on her dresser, Annie grimaced. Emma would not relish what was coming. "Emms, we need to talk."

"Now?"

Emma positioned herself to face Annie, and her rapid fire response spilled out. "Nope, no way. Mom said it's time to go, and besides, I wouldn't say I appreciate your tone or expression. Whatever you want to tell me cannot be good. Today is supposed to be good. Grab your sketchbook; we are out of here."

"Emma, we are going back in time."

"Yeah, Yeah, you've shared the spiel a million times of our far-flung adventures in the past."

The rise and fall sing-song tone of Emma's voice mocked Annie.

"Josh and I don't remember anything that transpired because we are not thirteen, and you think we are going back. Yup, I am very familiar with that song, but today I am not singing it. Save it for later. Time to go."

"Emma, we're going back today." Annie insisted.

Emma groaned. "Oh no. In case you have forgotten, this is supposed to be a day of celebration, an exciting day with lots of fun things for us to do. Pick another day for your fantasies."

"It's not a fantasy, and I don't pick the day. It picks me, it chooses us, and today is that day, like it or not. It's the Freedom House in the museum. The exhibit with the sculpture of the old woman in the rocking chair in the front. It's the portal for travel. Last night Missouri and Mamie were present at the cabin. It was a sign."

Emma crossed her arms in defiance. "I've tried to accept this mumbo jumbo because Mom, Gramby, and you have had some similar bonkers dreams. But honestly, Annie, I don't believe one word of it, and I am not going anywhere today except to the museum and then to that fancy hotel downtown."

"OK, you don't have to accept it. Just go with me to the Freedom House exhibit once all the outdoor ceremonies are over. If nothing happens, we'll just enjoy the day."

Emma sighed. "I guess you're going to drag Josh into this too."

"It will be the three of us the way it was before." Annie majestically announced. "It's all of us or none of us."

The day was clear and brilliant, indicative of the occasion. A hint of fall was in the air. Bright sunshine and a faint breeze made the outdoor seating layout a pleasant experience. Annie sketched the scenes of the day. On the left side of the stage sat a beaming Lonnie Bunch, the founding director of the National Museum of African American History and Culture. Beside him was John Lewis, the renowned congressman from Georgia, a living icon of the Civil Rights Movement. Directly in front of them sat President and Mrs. Bush and President and Mrs. Obama. The camera scanned the audience, and the large jumbotron screen revealed a who's who in America. President Clinton, Vice-President Biden, and his wife, Dr. Jill Biden. Colin Powell and dozens of others.

The speeches began one by one, starting with Reverend Calvin Butts, the historic Abyssinian Baptist Church pastor in Harlem. The dignitaries spoke in laudatory prose and praise of the day's significance. Robert DeNiro and Angela Bassett gave voice to the words of several historical Black icons. Will Smith and Oprah Winfrey repeated the exercise. President Bush called the museum "a national treasure" and "a commitment to truth." John Lewis said, *we may not have chosen the time, but the time has chosen us.*

Annie knocked her knee against Emma's to catch her attention. Arching her eyebrows and bobbing her head in a curt nod, she wanted Emma to acknowledge that she had uttered nearly the exact words earlier that morning. Annie considered it to be an affirmation of their destiny. And who wouldn't want to be validated by John Lewis?

President Obama delivered words of inspiration and passion. Annie sensed the presence of Mary, Fox, and countless other elders in his words. *"Too often we ignored, or forgot, the stories of millions upon millions of others, who built this nation just as surely, whose humble eloquence, whose calloused hands, whose steady drive, helped to create cities, erect industries, build the arsenals of democracy."*

She believed he spoke to her when he said, *"And for young people who didn't live through the struggles represented here, I hope you draw strength from the changes that have taken place. Come here and see the power of your own agency. See how young John Lewis was. These were children who transformed a nation in a blink of an eye. Young people come here and see your ability to make your mark."*

When President Obama concluded his remarks, the time had come in the program to ring the Emancipation or Freedom Bell. The bell was from the First Baptist Church of Virginia in Williamsburg, the earliest Baptist church established by African Americans. Ringing the bell was in remembrance of the chimes that rang out across the land as word of Abraham Lincoln's "Emancipation Proclamation" spread.

Ruth Odom Bonner, the daughter of Elijah Odom, a man born enslaved but who graduated from medical school after gaining his freedom, was selected to ring the bell. Her family joined Mrs. Bonner as she pulled the rope with the Obamas. The clapper struck the interior of the bell, and the boisterous sound of freedom echoed across the capital city.

After the bell ringing, the choir sang a stirring rendition of the Negro National Anthem, "Lift Every Voice and Sing."

Annie exchanged a glance with her mother at the last line, "True to our God, true to our native land." The passion they now shared for uncovering their family history and its connection to their native land was genuine and created a bond beyond the mother and daughter relationship. They shared a commitment to telling the story, comrades on a hallowed quest.

Numerous people had waited for this day, and it had finally arrived. The museum was officially open. Throngs eagerly made their way to the entrance. Annie observed Jay going through another doorway and ducked behind her grandfather, hoping she could remain inconspicuous. *No time for socializing. We need to be on our way.* Grabbing Emma and Josh's hands, she pulled them straight toward the level of the cabin's location.

"What's up"? asked Josh.

"We're traveling," whispered Annie.

"Awesome."

In a far cry from Emma's attitude, Josh wanted to believe, needed to believe he had traveled back in time. He rationalized that if he had encountered relatives from over a hundred years ago, perhaps he could one day go back to a time before his father died and be with him again, if only for a brief while. Or at least Annie assumed he wished it; she never approached the subject with him, but occasionally he made comments that suggested as much.

The trio hurried up the ramp carrying them to Freedom House.

"Now what?" asked Emma.

"Now this."

Annie wasn't sure what would happen as she reached into her purse and pulled out a carving of the small bird, but she hoped it might help.

"Where did that come from?" asked Josh.

"There was a gallery near Howard University with Black art and African artifacts. These carvings were in the window, and I swear, this Sankofa summoned me as if it were a talisman from the Ancestors. As soon as I glanced at it, I realized that it would be key to transporting us to the past once more. I asked Dad if I could have it, and predictably, he launched into the legend of the Sankofa; how our past is the key to our future. Naturally, he bought it for me."

Before Annie could continue, she spotted Jay approaching them. She took a deep breath attempting to appear laidback while contemplating a suggestion they catch up at a later time and place. But his smooth, appealing voice drove her to Fantasy Island, and she lost all perspective on how to remove him from their presence.

"I was hoping to catch up with you. We could pick up where we left off last night if you're interested. Hi," Jay said to Emma and Josh.

"Hi," they answered in unison.

Annie introduced them, still wondering what her next step should be.

Jay resumed his conversation with Annie. Pointing to the carving in her hand, he reached out and took the bird.

"Hey, that's nice. It's a—"

Fearful of what might happen if Jay said the word, Annie stretched out her hand, trying to snatch the bird back. She screamed, but it was in vain as the word "Nooo" echoed in the unnatural wind.

She was too late. Jay finished his sentence.

"Sankofa."

The wooden slats of the cabin began to rattle, and a tornado-like wind drew the four youngsters into the structure. A burst of light exploded. Annie, Emma, Josh, and Jay Anders were transported to 1935.

Chapter 7

Jim Crow

*T*his race is a cruel and curious species. They conceived a nation based on freedom while molding that nation into a system of injustice. These men and women attempt to sanitize the evils of genocide and slavery by dehumanizing their victims. They do this while proclaiming a belief in and feigning to worship a Higher Power. With a taste for meanness, they amuse themselves by mocking the oppressed. The tyrants emblazoned their bigotry with a name. They label it Jim Crow.

Before freedom and long after emancipation, jesters entertained the slavers by painting their faces with black cork. They sang, danced, distorted, and ridiculed those persecuted and held in bondage. They forged a stereotype that would follow Black men and women in America into modern times. Like so many other things, they purloined the character, Jim Crow. The trite, black-face caricature imitated a black minstrel who crooned the tune:

> "Wheel about and turnabout and do just so
> Every time I wheel about, I jump Jim Crow."

The performers did not disguise the intent of such foolery. White minstrels, most notably Thomas Daddy Rice, Jim Crow, put on shows constructed to demean and belittle. They portrayed the Black man as *a dim-witted buffoon incapable and unworthy of the talents and gifts bestowed on white men by the Creator. They distorted his appearance, making him gangly and unattractive. They dressed him in rags and depicted him as happy in his ignorance and servile state. They rationalized the loathsome treatment carried out against the people they enslaved through such portrayals.*

They concocted a plan to make their captives strike the world as less than human, so their inhumane treatment would vindicate the monocrats in their atrocities. It was a scheme designed to make the sons and daughters of Africa believe, as their persecutors did, that they were inferior and undeserving of compassion. The plan failed.

The arrogance and audacity of the oppressor empowered the enslaved who observed it to endure. While the credulous slavers popularized disparaging lies and underestimated the oppressed, the marginalized workers shielded their emotions and talents as a means of survival. Pretending to accept their fate, they learned, plotted, and stoically weathered the brutality.

When emancipation came, the struggle did not end. It began anew with similar atrocities constructed for the same results. The newly freed people were not shocked that the former slavers resisted the laws granting Black men and women liberty. They had studied well and anticipated it. They adapted as best they could.

After Reconstruction, Jim Crow became the symbol of renewed aggression towards Blacks as the children of Africa pursued their journey from freedom to independence. Southern lawmakers passed malevolent statutes to separate and hold them back. Their laws would segregate black from white and, in that separation, ensure that the former enslaved were given diminished opportunities in every aspect of life. They had substandard schools and inadequate medical care. Those in power stripped them of the newly acquired right to vote.

Intimidating Ambitious Negros became a common practice. They cultivated fields, only to have the lots wrenched from them, destroyed by fire or foreclosed upon. Many men suffered the indignation of lynching for minor or fabricated transgressions. Women recoiled with fear of being violated and abused. Still, there would be no deterrence of their resolve and resilience. Forging ahead, guided by the spirits of the Unknowns, the descendants remain covered and protected to this day. The ancestors bear witness from a spiritual plane. They are inconsolable, for as the people progress in this land, they move further from their history and ancestry, further from the conscious awareness of the motherland.

Thus, the Unknown Ancestors traverse the land of the living, abiding in the lives of their descendants. There can be no rest for the Unknowns as long as their descendants are not in harmony with their native land. They must do more than succeed; the scion must reclaim lost history.

Chapter 8

Freedom House

Simultaneously, four pairs of hands shot up protesting the ear-splitting rattle of the cabin timber. The floor beneath their feet vibrated, sending a surge through their bodies. A tornado pattern of gold dust swirled around them. The unexpected sensation lasted only a few seconds, but it could have been an hour to the frightened youngsters. The commotion ended, and the ensuing silence was almost scarier than the noisy transport.

Their surroundings revealed the cabin structure the mystical wind had drawn them into, but which was no longer the museum exhibit. A shabby shelter forged in an isolated, overgrown pasture had replaced the gleaming museum showcase. Since the life-size scale of the building display was no longer indoors, a gentle breeze rippled through the porous boards of the wooden cottage. The familiar scent of red Georgia clay wafted through the wind.

Annie, Emma, Josh, and Jay gazed out of the openings that passed for windows. Trees surrounded the perimeter of a clearing. A dirt road snaked toward a large red barn; the other paths spread to points unseen and unknown. In the distance, a dog barked, and the hum of bees melded into the air. The signs of a pending country spring, not a city fall, were all around.

With the upheaval over, Annie exhaled with the satisfaction that they had traveled as she had predicted and anticipated. She considered the problem Jay's presence presented and hesitated before daring to glance in his direction.

Jay stood confused and wide-eyed. He gazed at their surroundings, undeniably bewildered by what had happened and where they were.

"I knew it," shouted Josh, bouncing with enthusiasm. "I always believed we had time traveled, Annie, just the way you told us. I even remember forgetting if that makes any sense."

Annie's delight at being precise in her predictions was fleeting.

Shaking her head, Emma rotated slowly toward Annie, her face twisted in a fury.

Annie was at a loss for reacting to Emma's venomous expression. She could not recall an instance when Emma radiated such hostility. "Em's," she started.

But Emma did not let her finish. "With her voice trembling and growing louder with each word, Emma confronted her sister.

"I remember, too," Emma stuttered.

"I remember everything, Annie. I remember vile and disgusting men taking me. That didn't happen to you. It happened to me." She shouted, pounding her thumb in her chest.

Stepping closer to Annie, Emma shoved her sister. It happened so quickly, Annie lost her balance and dropped to the wooden floor.

"How could you do this to me, Ann? How could you bring me back here?"

Emma continued to advance on Annie with her fingers coiled tightly into fists. Annie sprang to her feet, glancing at Josh whose startled face conveyed what she was thinking. *Is Emma going to punch me?* Annie never considered Emma would have such a primal reaction to time-traveling again.

Shocked at the tears brimming in her sister's eyes, Annie stepped far enough away from Emma to avoid a potential fist striking her in the face. Throughout her ordeal in 1867, Emma never cried. When she was kidnapped and rescued, Emma was stoic and brave. Their ancestor Mary Jane said as much, describing Emma's fearlessness in standing up to the kidnappers.

Hoping to reassure Emma, Annie applied a new logic to their circumstances. "Well, technically, we're not back. We are not in 1867. I think we're in 1935."

"Check out the surroundings!" screamed Emma as the tears finally flowed. "This is Fox's cabin. This shack is where we were just before we went home the last time."

Annie surveyed the cabin, admitting inwardly it resembled the one from the past, though neglected and not inhabited for years.

Anna cautiously ventured closer to Emma, wrapping her hands around her sister's face.

"I promise you, Emms, nothing is going to happen to you this time. I will protect you."

Emma's arms spun out and pushed Annie's hands away. "The way you protected me the last time from Alden James and those criminals?"

"It wasn't Annie's fault that you and Mary Jane were kidnapped by the Klan when you went berry picking."

Josh's comments jolted Jay, finally provoking him to speak. "Are you crazy? What are the three of you talking about?"

"There," said Emma triumphantly, pointing to Jay. "You couldn't control bringing him along, and you can't control what's going to happen to us now any more than you could manage one iota of what happened before."

Torn between appeasing her sister and addressing the situation with Jay, Annie yielded to Jay's bewildered expression. She owed him an explanation now and would have to deal with Emma later.

"Can you please tell me what is going on? What just happened, and what do you mean we are in 1935?" Jay demanded.

Agonizing over her words, Annie haphazardly held up the Sankofa carving she had snatched from Jay's hand only moments before. She muddled through an explanation of the paraphysical impact the recitation of the name of the mystical Sankofa bird had on her, Emma, Josh, and now him, and their ability to travel through time. The only complication was that they didn't know how it worked, when it would work, or how to use it purposefully to transport to their own era.

She unraveled the implausible story of the three of them traveling the previous July to 1867, with a brief stop in 1912. She revealed the tale of the Unknown Ancestor and her family's crusade to uncover the details and identify one of their first ancestors from Africa. She was confident after the initial expedition to the past; they would visit again. Recently her senses had grown more intense, and she had come to believe they were destined for another journey soon, this time through the museum.

She promised Jay they would wind up back in 2016, at the museum and virtually little time will have passed. But she couldn't say how long they would be here in what she believed to be 1935. She gave a brief recap of Emma's near-disaster during their first trip, ending with an apology for placing him into the situation.

Jay rubbed the back of his neck, remembering the previous evening.

"Last night, when I approached you studying the São José Paquete, peculiar echoes were crying out from the ship. I assumed it was sound effects installed by the museum. But later, I asked my aunt, and she said it must have been the crowds and the excitement. Your expression now and last night proves I wasn't the only one listening to those cries. Your face was transcendent. Witnessing your reaction to the exhibit blew me away. You heard them."

Jay scowled as he confessed, "honestly, the voices have lived in that place since they first began bringing in the artifacts. I didn't dare mention it to anyone for fear they would believe I was psycho or think that the raw honesty of our ancestral history was too frightening for a kid and would stop allowing me to hang around. Geez, that's small potatoes compared to time travel".

Jay's emotions clashed with a combined sense of comprehension and resignation. "When I went home, I couldn't stop thinking about you and what happened at the museum. I figured I was just pumped to be talking to you finally. I wondered what kind of effect you had on me that I imagined the rocking chair in front of the cabin moving, although I was there when the workmen installed that exhibit using heavy-duty bolts to keep it stationary. I told myself it couldn't move. It happened, didn't it?"

Annie reluctantly nodded.

"I hate to interrupt this sweet little exchange," Emma broke in sarcastically, "but I want to remind you, this is dangerous, and we need to unravel the mystery of how to go home."

"If you remember, then you remember we have to find an ancestor, secure more information, and decipher the next clue," Annie said.

"I'm not leaving this cabin until I leave to go home," Emma declared. "Go find whatever long-lost relative you have to meet. Josh and I will stay in the cabin. After you finish, come back, yell Sankofa so we can clear out".

"I'm not staying here," Josh protested.

The arguments began anew as a shadow filled the door.

"My," said the young woman, "will you listen to all this ruckus?"

The four of them swiveled around to discover Mamie standing in the doorway. Annie rushed to hug her. Mamie arched her eyebrows expectantly at Josh and Emma as she squeezed Annie; both children ran to greet her.

"And who have we here?" she asked, regarding Jay.

"This is my friend, Jay Anders. Jay, this is our great-great-grandmother, Mamie Calhoun Jones."

"Not Jones yet, darlin'," she corrected. "Nice to meet you, Jay."

"You look exactly the way you did in 1912, but isn't it 1935? And why isn't your name Jones yet?"

"I assumed you understood that the calendar works kinda different with me when I am with you children. My part of your travels is peculiar. Just as before, I'm only a short stop on your way, in case you need a little water." She smiled and winked at Emma. "Or words to help you manage your heartache a bit," she continued, nodding at Josh and stroking his cheek. "But you've done your homework, and you're almost right. It's 1935 out there." Mamie gestured to the outside where her mother, Missouri, sat rocking in a chair perched on the cabin porch. It was reminiscent of the exhibit at the museum.

"Whoa," said Jay, "where did she come from?"

"That's my Mama, and today she is celebrating fifty years of marriage to Papa. She would tell you they've been good years, but not without pain and struggle, and unfortunately, they'll be a mite more sadness before she's called home to glory. But she would tell you too that's a part of living.

She craved some private time to call to mind those fifty years before the big party started. We should all do that sometimes," she said, glancing at the carving in Annie's hand. "Memories are important, and they are to be cherished. Even the difficult seasons of life should be appreciated because they guide our decisions, make us better, and prepare us for the future.

Reflections and memories are potent instruments. Sometimes they're so powerful they can move people through the ages, just like you children. Mama has been waiting for you. When you arrived at the cabin in the museum, the Unknown Ancestor spoke and declared the time had come for your next history lesson."

"I don't want to learn history this way," moaned Emma. "I'm afraid."

"I understand, baby, but the Unknowns are watching, and they will cover you."

Mamie then took the opportunity to study Jay. tilting her head, her body language implied she was listening to sounds only she could pick up, but Jay's head moved involuntarily as if he too was reacting to signals no one else could access. With a furrowed brow and a troubled expression, she reached for Annie's hand while keeping her eyes on Jay. "Safeguard your friend here."

A silent and cheerless exchange passed between Mamie and Jay.

Taking note of both Mamie's tone and the interaction between her great-great-grandmother and Jay, Emma glanced at Annie with an expression of smug confirmation that asserted; *you can't control what happens.*

The moment was interrupted by a voice coming from outside.

"Lord, Missouri, what are you doing out here? The party will soon start, and you are not even dressed yet."

A woman wearing a long, worn skirt with faint stains, a shirt that didn't match, and a bonnet with frayed sashes approached Missouri, smiling broadly.

"That's Claudia Hogan, my Mama's best friend since childhood. Her name was Meadows before she married. She's had some hard times; most everybody else has with this great depression they've been through.

My Papa's a stern man, some might even say selfish, and he doesn't give way much. He makes everyone pay for what they acquire from him, even his children. He has dozens of sharecroppers working his land in similar fashion to a white man. Papa doesn't suspect Mama packs up food baskets for Miss Claudia and her family and has the grandchildren take them down to her cabin. She tells them, 'Don't let Sweetie catch you now.' She always calls Papa, Sweetie. Mama will never talk bad about Papa, but she wishes he were more charitable. She tells all of us the Bible says, God loves a cheerful giver."

"Will she be at the party?" asked Emma.

"Not likely," answered Mamie softy, "not likely. There's ill will and family difficulties with Miss Claudia's sister Lilly. Listen closely later when my Mama recounts more of their story in her later reflections. Lilly married my brother Aquilla making Mamma and Papa are her in-laws. Claudia and Lilly's daddy, Mr. Jake, works down at the mill. He's white, but he owned up to them being his daughters. He helps out some with his grandchildren, Partner's children, Partner, is what folk call Aquilla.

Changing the subject, Mamie brightened. "You will be at the party, just not right away. Wherever Mama's memories take her before the party today, they will take you."

Claudia and Missouri's conversation brought the groups attention back to the women in the yard. Claudia Hogan was now sitting on the porch steps a few feet from Missouri's chair.

"Claudie, when Sweetie and I started courting, my older sister Ann had married the Newsom boy and was living in this very cabin where most of us were born. Sweetie and I would walk all over these acres, him talking about his big dreams and all that he was going to have and do. That Joshua Calhoun was one proud man, still is." She chuckled.

"But not too proud back then to admit to me that he could make his mark, but he couldn't read or write. We were fortunate. Papa made sure that all his children could read and write. May Jane said it was because a girl named Annie passed through here after the War between the States and told him everyone, even us girls, should be able to read and write. Imagine old Fox listening to some young girl.

"Anyhow, Sweetie said that was what he admired about my daddy. Fox McElmurry made sure all his children, even the girls, went to school. We younger ones went to Lincoln Grammar School. The older kids went to Lewis High School, named for my Papa's old friend General John Lewis of the Freedmen's Bureau. You remember how Papa loved to tell stories. He would talk about General Lewis long after he left Macon and the Freemen's Bureau and went to Atlanta and became the first superintendent of schools for all of Georgia.

"I was too young to remember when that girl Annie came through here. But Papa would tell how May Jane and that girl's sister Emma disappeared one day, and General Lewis helped find them. There was a boy with them too. His name was Joshua, same as Sweetie. My Mama said nobody ever touched my daddy along the same line as those young kids. We owe our schooling, and that Papa treated the girls the same as the boys to them. Mama said after their visit, he was always hopeful about the future of the Negro, no matter what old Jim Crow wrought. He would say one day, a colored man with an African name was going to be President of these United States."

Both women shook their heads in disbelief and chuckled. Astonished by their influence over their ancestors, the children glowed with pride.

"Whatever happened to Lewis High School?" Claudia asked.

"In '76, someone set fire to it. Some people didn't favor having all the colored children learn to read and write. After two years and five thousand dollars in insurance money, a new school opened. In 1887, Mr. Stephen Ballard from Brooklyn, New York, donated a large sum of money to the school, and a new building went up along with a girls' dormitory. General Lewis gave his permission to rename the school The Ballard Normal School. It was relocated to a bigger campus in 1911. My children and now my older grandchildren are Ballard graduates or students. The little ones are at Holly Grove Elementary. Graduates of Ballard Normal can go right into teaching after graduation if they choose."

"But Mr. Josh didn't go to school."

"No, neither Lewis nor Ballard were ever public schools, and they charged a fee. That was a luxury most colored folks couldn't afford. The government didn't start public schools for colored children in Macon until 1872. And even then, the colored schools couldn't take everyone. They were too crowded, and most children needed to work in the fields or find other ways to help their families. I never became a schoolteacher, though a few of my sisters did. But I became Sweetie's teacher and taught him to read and write.

I had a dowry of fifty acres when I got married, but Papa told Sweetie marrying a woman who could read and write was more valuable than the land. Sweetie put a lot of hard work into learning to read, cultivating the land, and hiring the workers he needed. Old Jim Crow has tried to stop us now and then, but Sweetie kept pushing. Kept on telling the children to learn from him but especially from old Fox and Mary."

"He couldna done it without you, Missouri."

Touched by the loyalty of her long-time friend, Missouri reached down and patted her hand. "We did it jointly, and today I have the joy of my memories. I take genuine pleasure in reflecting on the past.

. My father was born under the cloud of slavery. Still, he never used it as an excuse to withhold anything from his children. He and my mother are the cornerstone of everything I believe and everything I have taught my children," said Missouri

"Papa would sit under a blue sky and warm sun tellingall kinds of stories, mostly to teach us lessons. My brother Amos had a favorite one about a bird. Papa said it was a story passed down from Africa that he learned on the plantation before freedom. The bird had to learn the lesson of the importance of reflecting on the past. By remembering where she came from, he would say, she understands and appreciates where she is going."

"What kind of bird was it?" Claudie asked.

"I'm not sure what kind of bird it was. I only remember its name. He called it …"

Chapter 9

Time Hopping

Missouri's attention drifted to fond and distant memories of her childhood, sitting by the fire with her brothers and sisters eating pecans. Amused by recollections of her father's rich storytelling, she chuckled and wistfully drifted into a private reverie of Fox's tales and her brother Amos's favorite story of the mythical African bird.

Claudie called her name, drawing her back to the conversation, and a grin of genuine delight spread across Missouri's face. She pictured her father's affable grin and answered her friend's question. "He called the bird Sankofa."

Her proclamation of the word Sankofa activated the now-familiar yet inexplicable movement through the ages for the young adventurers. Instantaneously, the four time-travelers migrated to yet another era, and they found themselves planted on a dusty road adjacent to a railroad track. Dry, brittle grass swayed around them as they peered into the distance. They spotted a train moving away toward its next destination. Its doleful whistle emphasized their isolation in a new place and probably another stretch of history.

"Dang," exclaimed a disheveled Josh, brushing the dust from his clothes. "We have to figure out how to knock off the unexpected shout-outs of Sankofa, or at least anticipate when it's going to happen. This hasty time-shifting cannot be good for our internal organs."

Josh's pseudo-medical diagnoses were commonplace to Annie and Emma, and the girls exchanged glances and snickered. Annie relaxed at the matter-of-fact sisterly connection, believing that for the time being, she and Emma were at a détente.

She was wrong.

Sensing Annie loosening up, Emma shot her a cold-eyed frown. She thrust out her chin, steeling her resolve not to allow Annie to deceive her again and convince her everything was fine. She would not be so quick to trust her sister once more in dangerous and unfamiliar circumstances.

Jay observed the interaction between the sisters and their mockery of Josh's solemn nature. He surmised Josh was regularly in the minority around his female cousins and the target of their teasing. Deciding Josh needed to appreciate he could count on him as an ally, Jay draped his arm around the younger boy's shoulder.

"Hey bro, it's cool. I don't think these blasts are something I'll become accustom to anytime soon, either. And I'm going to have a problem figuring out what year it is whenever we skip through time." Jay suddenly stopped talking, taking stock of what he was wearing.

"Holy cow. Our clothes are different."

Jay and Josh wore gray faded overalls and shirts of a darker shade. Emma and Annie had on oversized dresses covered by aprons.

"This is weird. Did it happen before?" Jay asked.

The three nodded in unison.

"Not only do our clothes change, but items such as plastic water bottles, cell phones, anything indicative of the twenty-first century don't travel either," Annie told him.

Jay patted his side and back pockets, hoping to locate his phone.

Annie flashed a smug expression and told him not to bother. "Your phone will resurface after we're back in the twenty-first century, whenever that is."

"What other kinds of things happened?"

Happy to have a male partner, Josh was eager to tell Jay of the adventures of 1912 and later 1867, but Annie interrupted. "We can't stay here. We can talk as we walk, but we must keep moving. We should follow the tracks. They will take us to someplace where there are people."

Jay was still for a moment. "There is a town east of our location; we need to move in that direction. Let's go."

The three hesitated briefly but took Jay at his word.

Starting the long trek to a new location, a degree of comfort settled over the tiny legion of voyagers. The Georgia humidity released the girls' natural curls, tamed earlier by the flat iron. Emma remembered the initial long walk during their first journey to the past, beginning at the Martin Luther King Jr. Memorial. It was a hot day in July, and they were thirsty. They met Mamie along the way, and she gave them the most refreshing water Emma had ever tasted. It was weird how everything she had forgotten over the past three months was now so crystal clear.

Before long, the small band of travelers reached a town. They were surprised as they approached to discover a bustling city and clear signs, they were beyond 1867. Still, they didn't think it was 1935. They faced a labyrinth of buildings concurrent with the early years of twentieth-century Georgia. There were carts and ox-drawn wagons, but the cityscape included streetcars and automobiles as well. People strolled along outfitted in attire suitable for the early twentieth century. Wide crinolines were gone. Simplicity was prevalent for nearly all the women, although it was easy to distinguish the more affluent citizens by the trimmings and elaborate accessories on their garments.

The four moved cautiously along the sidewalk without a destination in mind. Anticipating telltale signs of the era, they were anxious to discover when and where they were and what the Unknown had in store for them. Distracted by their conversation and exploration, they paid no mind to the white male coming toward them. Jay made the inexcusable blunder of a Black male in the south, neglecting to step aside as the man neared.

The presumption of privilege was swift as the man grabbed Jay and raised his walking cane to strike the teen. Jay's head snapped as he peered directly at his attacker with the intent of protesting. Annie clutched his arm and instructed him in a frantic whisper to drop his head and avert the man's soulless eyes. Jay's instinct was to resist, but the fear in Annie's voice stopped him. It happened so quickly; they did not anticipate the elderly Black man rushing to their rescue, but they were relieved as he intervened.

"Please, sir, the boy is slow, and he didn't mean no harm. I promise you I will take care of him myself as soon as we arrive at home."

The man hesitated momentarily and finally let Jay go with a shove. Jay lowered his head and remained silent at Annie's muttered and desperate pleadings for him to keep his mouth shut.

"I have dealt with your kind before, boy, meandering on the sidewalk when a white man passes. But eventually, your sort runs up against men who won't tolerate your obstinance or who rely on others to handle it I fix that arrogance on the chain gang every day," he mocked.

Annie frantically whispered in Jay's ear, who bitterly answered, "Sorry, sir."

The group remained silent. Their eyes averting the offended man and each other until he was out of sight. Jay rapidly inhaled and exhaled, rubbing sweaty palms against his pants. His palpable anger was visible to the others as he absorbed what had happened. The incident and his forced response were against his twenty-first-century nature in every way possible. His parents taught him to stand and be proud as a Black man and to cower to no one. Yet to do less here and now could put his life, and the lives of his friends, in jeopardy.

Eager to to thank the gentleman who intervened, Annie's words caught in her throat realizing who was standing before her. The man had aged since she'd last seen him, but there was no mistaking the dimpled cheeks and drowsy eyelids. When they'd parted, he had just finished the bedtime story about the frightened bird who learned to appreciate her self-worth by remembering how much her family and village loved her. The person standing before her was part of her loving village of the past, and there was no forgetting her great-great-great-great-grandfather. She reached out to Fox McElmurry, squeezing his hand.

Fox gazed at the children with undisguised affection. "Well, sir, I never figured you children would come back to these parts again.

"Where are we?" inquired Josh.

"Macon, Georgia," Fox replied. "Though a lot has changed in these parts since you were last here." "But it's only been three months since Annie told us about our visit," said Josh.

Baffled by Josh's comments, Fox inquired why Annie had to tell them about their first visit. Josh explained that he and Emma had no recollection of their earlier experience once they returned to their own time. But now that they had been sent back in time once again, their memories of the first experience were as vivid as Annie's. And like before, they were time hopping. He continued, explaining they made a stop before this one on Missouri and Joshua's wedding anniversary.

Fox shook his head in amazement. "Three months for you. A whole lot more for me."

"If it's a lot more for you, then events have transpired that might contain valuable information. Tell us t what happened after you registered to vote in 1867," begged Annie.

"After you young'uns visit, Mary and I had two more children, a son Johnny, and a little girl we named Emma," he said, smiling at Emma.

"Over the years, Mary and I welcomed other travelers, but none such as you. As our children grew up, some of them hosted travelers as well, especially Ann."

Fox then focused on the young man he'd rescued on the street.

"And who might this be?" he inquired.

"My name is Jay Anders, and I am a friend of Annie's. I was with these guys when I recognized the carving Annie was holding. I heard your daughter say she is well-known to you, and you tell stories about her", he joked as his lips curled into a smile. "She's popular in my family too. When I mentioned her by name, we all got sucked into the travel vortex, me by accident."

Fox chuckled. "Things always were peculiar with you kids."

Speaking directly to Jay, he continued, "But not much about traveling is by accident, son. I learned that over the years."

Scrutinizing Jay intently, Fox continued. "You have a gift. You hear things, things that are silent in the wind to other folks, isn't that right?"

"Yes, sir. A lot more lately," he added seriously.

"It's not more, just that circumstances probably make you extra aware. You keep right on listening and listen closely. It can keep you out of a heap of trouble."

Unable to contain his curiosity, Josh interrupted to inquire about the year.

Fox contemplated how to respond to Josh's question. "Time stopped for me a while back, Joshua, so the years have little meaning for me."

The group was reluctant to ask Fox what he meant, so they simply followed as Fox strolled away from the city center.

"So, you say Joshua and Missouri were celebrating their anniversary? How many years?" asked Fox.

"Fifty," replied Annie.

"Fifty years married," he murmured.

"Joshua Calhoun had more ambition and determination than anyone I ever met. I speck he is one of the most prosperous colored men in Macon by now. He was well on his way when I moved on. I accumulated a bit of land myself and gave each of my girls a dowery. More important, Mary and I sent the children to school. They stayed close to these parts. Ann became a teacher, mainly cause of you, Annie. But the next group, including some of Missouri and Joshua's kids, started moving away as Jim Crow laws took over Georgia and every place else.

Good people are trying to make a difference, but still, I think these are troubled times for colored folks. You kids need to be careful and stay out of the way of men like that fella you just ran into. Jay's gift will help you if he respects its power and heeds its warnings."

Annie didn't ask Fox where he moved on to since his last encounter with Joshua Calhoun. Emma and perhaps Josh may not have understood his meaning, but it was clear to her. She inquired instead what happened in Macon and Lizella after she, Josh, and Emma went back and asked him to share details of the family's story after that.

"After Reconstruction faded away, white folks sought retribution for what they supposed was taken from them. They backpedaled on colored people's right to vote, charged poll taxes, and made people pass reading tests to vote. They decided too many of us were serving on juries and running and winning elected office. They stopped all of that. There was a play called *The Clansman*, 'bout a colored man trying to court a white woman. That led to made-up stories about colored men and white women. There were riots up in Atlanta. A bunch of folks died. Like I said, troubled times, but nothing could be worse than slavery, so I guess we have to keep moving forward despite all the troubles."

Fox glanced at the Sankofa carving in Annie's hand and gently reached for it. Closing his eyes, he muttered an incantation over the bird and handed it back to Annie. Fox instructed her to keep it in a safe place and not to lose it.

"What was that?"

"Just a prayer of sorts I learned from an African fella a long time ago."

Fox pointed to a church in the distance and gestured for the children to follow the road. Annie recognized the church as the community gathering center when Emma and Mary Jane went missing. The church congregation must have updated it, for there was an addition.

"Aren't you coming?" implored Emma.

Fox shook his head. "No, baby, there are some lines I can't cross."

He spoke gently to Annie and Josh. My children are all grown up now with kids of their own. I can't say if they will remember you or not, but they will welcome you. Ann is probably expecting you."

Jay said to Fox, "There is crying and grief there. It's so intense; words can't describe it."

The others faced the church as the doors opened, and a crowd of mourners emerged. Six men were carrying a simple coffin and processed to a graveyard at the side of the church. A woman following behind them clutched a noose to her breast. Annie prepared to ask Fox whose funeral they were attending, but he was no longer present. Gazing beyond the church grounds, Annie froze as she recognized the woods from her dream.

Chapter 10

The Red Summer

*C*ontrary to the illusion of bright sun and lazy blue skies, 1919 will be labeled The Red Summer, an allegory for the bloodshed on American soil. The "War to End All Wars" is done, but it has not brought peace to the American Negro. Their fight neither began nor does it conclude with World War I. It did not originate with the allied nations they defended and fought with in Europe and Japan. The Negro's war was launched on the shores of Africa hundreds of years before. It began in the land from which their ancestors were captured then shifted to this country, where they would build and propel a nation to economic dominance.

The Negro's naiveté led them to believe military service would deliver the respect they coveted. But they fought with no parallel compensation or recognition to that of white soldiers. Negro soldiers repatriated to their homeland from the war as despised as when they departed. There are no raucous celebrations. No victory parades or dignified honor guards to welcome these warriors home. Negro soldiers will carry on as best they can to put their lives back together without assistance from the government. Their trials and tribulations will persist for generations to come.

The great migration has begun. Negros are leaving the South in search of better lives elsewhere. But no place is veritably safe for them. There are few jobs or opportunities for Negro veterans. The Red Summer *is a season of singular violence as riots spread across the country; in the Yankee-proud North, the independent Midwest, and the blighted South. Depraved mobs in the North and Midwest burn Negro churches, lodges, and homes. Their Southern counterparts burn and torment Negro men, women, and children.*

It is an age of lawlessness with no system to safeguard the bloodline from the mob violence of small and large assemblies. The absence of justice is stark. The freedom and progress of formerly enslaved people threaten those who need to authenticate superiority. Persecution continues. Accused, hunted, tortured, and killed, ofttimes on the same day, Negros must be vigilant against a backdrop of bigotry while searching for some pretense of fairness.

The spirits of the Unknowns lament across time and space. Divination warns the living of approaching dangers. Beware. Run. Hide. The descendants do not discern the origin of an abrupt awakening, or the source of the faint and ominous whispers carried through the trees. Nonetheless, they sense the peril, and instinct warns them to be cautious. Souls who have experienced danger throughout their lives listen with their hearts as well as their heads. Beware. Run. Hide.

For a wayward glance, a stolen apple, an uppity cadence, or the mere crime of being Black in the wrong place at the wrong time, our descendants are tortured and hung. The children are robbed of a carefree childhood and must conform to a subservient image conceived by inferior men. The elders teach them to grovel in the presence of Whites. Frightened girls and women shrink into oblivion to avoid violation.

The resurgence of the Ku Klux Klan strikes new fears among the people. Scapegoats for every form of frustration, more than four thousand reported lynchings of Black people will take place across Southern states over several decades. No one can accurately state the number of these casualties of this uncommon war.

My soul agonizes for my descendants victimized by the violence fueled by bitterness. As is true throughout our people's history in this country, the masses suffer cruelty they have not earned. Deprived of the meager protections afforded during Reconstruction, the fight for justice is a crusade the sons and daughters of Africa must wage with scant help from the powerful. But from the land of Sasha, the Unknowns will assist our descendants in whatever manner possible. The spirit presence warns of perils; the gifts of sight and sound are among powers Unknowns can bestow to protect our seed. The girl has the advantage of sight. The boy responds to voices soundless to others. May the Orisha protect them. May our gifts be sufficient.

Chapter 11

The Calhouns

Outfitted in his olive drab, Army-issued uniform, Private Early Lee Calhoun stood ramrod straight. The garrison cap sat atop his head. The canvas belt cinched tightly around his waist, and the hob-nailed boots beneath the puttee leg-wraps circling his trousers brandished the wear and tear of war. He made a striking image standing at attention, and Missouri Calhoun gazed lovingly at her son with pride.

Early Lee returned to Georgia from France on the USS Powhatan after serving in the 327th Labor Battalion Company A. The young soldier never hazarded a guess his homecoming would involve performing the duties of pallbearer for Paul Jones' funeral. The lawless practice of lynching stood distant and unthinkable to him during the months he'd spent in Europe. Woodrow Wilson labeled World War I the "war to end all wars," but evidently, that label pertained only to foreign nations. *I guess he wasn't referring to the war raging against the Negro in his own country*, Early mused.

Wilson proclaimed in his War Declaration, "the world must be made safe for Democracy." Activist A Philip Randolph retorted, "We would rather make Georgia safe for the Negro." Early had no doubt which principle triumphed. Georgia, nor any other place in the United States for that matter, was genuinely safe for Black men.

Envisioning the heinous violence of the past few days, he focused on the contempt and hatred most white folk held towards his race. So much hate, it would drive them to torch a man and then hang him. He masked inner rage, taking deep breaths to settle his nerves. Had this been what his grandparents witnessed during slavery? Had his parents succeeded in sheltering them from the worst of such savagery? He was not naïve about the racism of Georgia, but this implied an evil deeper than racial contempt.

Early Lee brooded over how different life would have been if he had remained in France. Nothing could have kept him from returning to his wife, the former Ella Mae Bevins, and he'd missed his close-knit family during his tour in Europe. But if he'd stayed, he could have sent for Ella Mae, and calamities like this one would be distant events in a faraway land. But his brothers and sisters were his rock. Early would endure the racial animosity of America because he belonged here. Georgia was home despite all its failings. He wasn't so gullible to fantasize that America would be substantially different for colored soldiers and veterans after the fighting. Still, he had hoped things would be better. The lack of progress for colored people threw cold water on his homecoming.

No, the war didn't change the nation's attitude toward the Negro, as many had hoped. But combat transformed many Negro soldiers. A hefty number of Early's companion Black soldiers remained in Paris when the conflict ended, choosing exile over the mindless racism in America. They often spoke of the conditions in the states, but when the moment came to decide whether to go home or not, some of Early's best buddies stunned him with their decision to say in Europe. There were rumors of thousands choosing to give up the land of their birth, the country for which they'd fought, rather than go back. Others returned committed to challenging the status quo.

Muffled sounds drew Early's attention back to the present. He studied his brothers, Aquilla, the oldest, Noah, Ernest, and Martin, the youngest. They jokingly called Martin "Doc" because he bragged nonstop about his plan to study dentistry. Aquilla farmed, following in their father's footsteps. Early was aware that her children leaving Georgia distressed Missouri, but she accepted Noah's plan to abandon Lizella. He believed Chicago held better prospects for him. Ernest persisted in his calling to the ministry. Early glanced at his cousins and neighbors. It could have happened to any one of them.

As with so many other Black men facing lynch mobs across the South, the law charged Paul Jones with attacking a white woman. Early didn't believe it. He concluded it was fabricated justification for the violence used to suppress the burgeoning spirit of colored people. *Keeping us in our place*, he thought bitterly.

Paul's detention rapidly spiraled out of control after his arrest. The plan was for the sheriff to take him before a judge. Before that happened, a mob of at least four hundred men descended on the jail. They were no match for the sheriff. Beyond that, no one expected the sheriff to protect a colored prisoner from a crowd, including the sheriff's neighbors and friends.

They were right. The mob dragged Paul out of jail, and someone in the group shot at him. Others followed suit, puncturing his body with bullet wounds. However, gunfire didn't kill him. Paul was still alive when the ringleaders doused him with oil and set him on fire. They eventually hung him, his agonizing screams slicing through the night air. The putrid odor of burning flesh would not soon drift away nor be forgotten.

Good men and women recoiled behind closed doors, attempting to blot out the sounds of the brutalizing violence and the suffering of a man born in the area, living and working among them until unimaginable horror struck, battering the fragile peace of the populace.

Frightened any family could be wrongfully targeted, the Calhouns joined other households in locking their doors and hiding away. Even the mighty Joshua Calhoun abandoned the pretense of courage in the face of such malice. He and the others understood how the mob viewed them. They were coloreds in need of punishment for the crime of being Black.

Early continued his survey of those around him, and his scrutiny came to rest on the stern man standing beside his mother. Joshua Calhoun's blank expression obscured whatever beliefs wended through his mind. Bibb County's paragon of success, Calhoun relished being distinguished, respected, and feared.

The farmers sharecropping on his land who dared not miss a payment to Mister Josh were in awe of him. He intimidated his children and grandchildren as well. This noble Black man, farmer, and businessman who owned hundreds of acres of debt-free land was, in the end, no different than all the others. With his prominence and all he had accomplished; he was no match for Jim Crow and the murderers of Paul Jones.

Perhaps it was the times, or just the man himself, but Joshua ruled his family with an iron fist, and few crossed him. Born in Byron, Georgia, he kept his distance from his parents and siblings after his marriage to Missouri. In the same way, he discouraged Missouri's family relationships though she managed to sidestep his efforts to limit her family contacts. Her brother Johnny lived nearby, and her sister Frances was adept at outflanking Josh's manipulation. He had many acquaintances and business associates but few friends. His grandchildren would remember him as cold and unapproachable.

Annie, Emma, Joshua, and Jay lurked in the shadows, conscious of intruding on the solemn procession to the carefully tended cemetery behind the church. They followed discreetly, stopping at a distance for the grave-side service as the pallbearers placed the simple coffin in the ground. The minister spoke his final words, and the crowd dispersed.

The men, clustered in small groups, murmured about the events of the past twenty-four hours. The ladies tended to the Jones family and set out food donated they would serve at the repast.

The youngsters were uncertain of what to do next until a woman with large misty eyes approached. Her plump apple cheeks warmed as she placed her arm around Annie's shoulder.

"Child, last you were in Lizella, we were pert-near the same age." She chuckled.

Tears bubbled over from the woman's eyes and flowed down her cheeks. She embraced a shocked Annie. The teen was unsure if the tears were for the man just buried or the bond that had formed between the two when they first met at a family picnic. For Annie, a mere three months had passed. For Ann McElmurry Newsom, fifty-two years had gone by since she met the young girl who would bear her name one day.

Annie was stupefied by the presence of the woman grinning at her. A wry expression crossed Ann's face.

"I guess you're wondering why I'm not more surprised you're here." She laughed. Ann barged ahead with her tale before Annie could respond.

"Well, now that's quite a story. One day a stranger showed up at my house talking real crazy about being my kin from the future. I sent one of my kids to fetch Papa, who came right away.

"Papa and the man stepped away so I couldn't eavesdrop on their conversation., though Papa wasn't any too surprised he was there. He talked to that fella as if they'd been friends for years. They finally shook hands, and that man walked into the wheat fields, passing over the horizon. He disappeared before my eyes. I swore it was a haint."

Annie, Emma, and Josh's facial expressions contorted in confusion, but Jay broke in, explaining that Ann was speaking of a ghost.

"Papa sat me down and told me the story of the Travelers. People moving through time with gifts and powers from the African gods, gathering information about their ancestors and the forebearers who were first brought here on slave ships.

I worried he was losing his mind until he told me the three of you traveled from the future. It all made sense to me then; how you suddenly came out of nowhere and then went away just as mysteriously. But more than the coming and going, it was how you spoke and what you said about the books you had at your house. You told me you all went to school as if that were the most natural thing in the world. Papa believed you could come back one day, although he had never met any Traveler more than once, and none quite like you. He said you were special, though I already figured that."

"Well, Papa's favorite pastime was telling stories, so after time went by and you didn't come back, I figured maybe he had made it all up. But I prayed it was true anyhow. I always hoped we would meet again to thank you for talking to Papa about girls needing to read and write. My brothers and sisters, and I went to school. Some in the next generation are even going to college."

Ann choked on her final words. She reached out and wrapped Annie in an embrace and sighed. Stepping back, she shook her head sadly. "I'm sorry the Unknown chose such a sad day to send you back, but I guess that's part of your destiny. I am happy you're here, and I will do what I can while you are here to help continue your search for the answers you seek."

Ann could always recognize a hungry child, and, noting Josh's longing eyes wandering to the spread laid out for the mourners, she suggested they walk over to where the women were serving plates heaped with food.

"Won't someone ask who we are?" questioned Jay.

"No one in these parts questions who attends a funeral," said Ann, giving Jay the once over.

"I don't believe I've had the pleasure of meeting you. Are you kinfolk?"

Approaching the mourners, Annie quickly introduced Jay as a friend and explained how he happened to be with them when the Unknown swept them into the past.

Ann gave her young namesake a wink, moving her naturally curved eyebrows upward.

Amused that circumstanced exposed Annie's interest, Jay radiated his sunny temperament.

Annie's cheeks burned with embarrassment as she attempted to change the subject, mortified that Ann had so easily picked up on her attraction to Jay. She tried asking about various cousins they'd met on their first journey, but Ann was having none of it.

Looping her arm through Jay's, she targeted her full attention on the young man. "Now, tell me all about yourself, Jay. Do you do well in school?"

Annie groaned. "Mom might as well be here."

"I'll take that as a compliment," bantered Ann.

Ann led the four to the women, dressed in black and standing behind long tables. They were filling plates and greeting guests with kind eyes and warm words. "These are my sister Missouri's daughters, Sophia, Lila, Gertrude, and Mamie. Mamie is due to have a baby any day now." Annie beamed at Mamie, expecting a warm welcome, but was disappointed when the woman showed no sign of recognition.

"Mamie's time swaps differ from Ann's. In real-time, she is unable to recall who you are or your relationship to her," said Jay.

"You've only been at this a few hours, and you can perceive the complexities of our family dynamics. How is that possible?

"The voice. Now that I'm tuned in, it's more distinct. I realize what Fox meant when he told me to pay attention. It is also clearer why the Unknowns drew me into the vortex to travel with you guys. My gift, as they call it, is an asset. A force is revealing information you might otherwise not have. Like the distinct sound of Josh's stomach growling, means he's ready to eat."

It was a traditional Georgia meal, with plenty to go around. They feasted on greens, chicken, crackling bread, and lemonade while settling into greeting family members and neighbors from the surrounding area. Jay and Annie became better acquainted as they settled into a cozy union. Mamie busied herself with two small children, though she occasionally eyed Annie with curiosity.

As the day ended and people began to leave, Emma grew anxious, pressing Annie to a way to bring the excursion to an end. Annie was unconvinced their mission was complete, but she had let Emma down once, and she wouldn't do it again. The carving and the museum played a role in the travel. She would come back on her own, without Emma. Her sister's anxiety was spiraling, and Annie intended to make things right with her. She withdrew the small carving from her pocket and asked Ann how to use it to propel them back to their own time. Annie dismissed the notion of speaking the bird's name aloud for fear it would push them to another time and place instead of home.

Ann folded her hands around Annie's and hesitated, unsure how to answer. "The Unknown has graced this figure with exceptional powers, and it will factor into your trip home. But not tonight. Tonight, you will stay with my mother. Tomorrow, Jay and Josh will learn what how it is to work in the fields. Emma will attend school, and you will have a rare experience."

Ann intended to add more to her explanation of what was to happen, but before she could finish, she, along with the others, watched perplexed as the color drained from Emma's face. Emma's knees buckled; she flopped to the ground and passed out cold.

Chapter 12

Dance, Emma Dance

Annie sank to the grass beside Emma's crumpled form and gently stroked her sister's head of massive curls. Her grandmother was mistaken. The Unknown should not have dispatched Emma to the past the first time, and now they repeated the error. *I made matters worse by insisting she come back and not telling anyone what happened in 1867. If mom and dad had an inkling of the mortal danger Emma faced, they would not only have forbidden me from taking her, but they also wouldn't have let any of travel to the past again.*

Grimacing at the old clapboard church, she concluded the facts were indisputable. The peaceful rustle of trees pushed by gentle winds disguised the reality of their situation. This place and time were not safe. Annie was incapable of guaranteeing they would be out of harm's way. It was almost a certainty there would be risks. The sentimental attachment to history and the past was her fascination, not Emma's and not Josh's. Annie quickly reached a decision. The others would vault back to 2016, while she remained until she obtained the answers she was fated to discover.

Annie blinked back tears and stammered sorrowful regrets begging Emma to wake up. The older Ann knelt beside Annie, lightly pushing her aside. Pressing a cold cloth on Emma's forehead and cooing soothingly, she brought the child back to consciousness.

Convinced Emma was uninjured, Annie asked to speak to Ann, leaving Emma in Mamie's care.

"Emma, Josh, and Jay must return to our time as soon as possible. I understand you believe they belong here now, but I disagree. I should have come alone".

Shoving the wooden carving into Ann's hand, she continued. "Take this and send them home. Fox recited a prayer over this figure of the Sankofa. Its supernatural powers brought us to the past; I believe the prayer reinforced the powers making them stronger. Fox had a unique gift from the ancestors, and you have it as well. Please perform a travel spell on them or whatever it takes so I can pursue this without endangering my family and my friend."

Annie was unaware that Josh and Jay were standing close behind her.

"I'm not going anywhere," Josh snapped.

"Neither am I," echoed Jay.

Facing the indignant boys, Annie stood her ground. "Josh, you're not thirteen. That's the age of all true Travelers."

"Not True. Emma and I have traveled, and we are not thirteen. Gramby said the Unknown doesn't make mistakes, and I believe that. Just because you haven't figured out yet why we're here doesn't mean we don't belong."

Folding her arms in defiance, Annie declared, "It's my responsibility to explore the family history. I am the key to solving the mystery of the Unknown".

"Says who, Miss hotshot?" Josh snapped back.

Ignoring Josh, Annie addressed Jay. This quest is not about your family; it's not your crusade. You belong in the twenty-first century enjoying the museum opening with your family. You're all going back, and that's the end of it."

Jay's temper flared.

"Stop and consider how presumptuous you sound."

"Everything spoken of the Unknown Ancestor foreshadows a predetermined destiny for particular travelers. The way I see it, the decision of who comes or goes isn't yours, Annie. There is a point to all of us being here, whether you agree with it or not. Besides, I would be crazy to pass up an opportunity such as this, even with the understanding it could be dangerous. Besides that, I enjoy being with you," He concluded with a wink.

Irate at Jay's caviler attitude, Annie reviewed again why everyone needed to leave.

The argument escalated until Mamie ordered them to hush. She gingerly helped Emma to her feet as Ann took the distressed girl by the hand.

"It's time for us to go for a walk, baby."

Annie took steps to join them, but Mamie seized her arm to stop her. "They won't go far, and that walk is not part of your journey." There was a familiarity in her words taking Annie by surprise. "You recognize me?" asked Annie, perplexed.

"I know when my aunt has business to take care of," replied Mamie. Her unflinching expression stopped Annie from going further as Emma and Ann ambled towards the meadow. The limitless landscape spread before her, calling to mind the pastured land from her dreams. Trusting Mamie, she made no further attempt to follow her sister.

A dull smokey haze rolled in and began to block the group's view. They studied the older woman and slender girl as they faded from sight and into the horizon and were no longer visible.

Ann meandered aimlessly, humming a tune and pointing out varieties of wildflowers and birds to Emma. Gold-winged butterflies flitted through the field, and pollen particles drifted in the air. Emma was content to listen and stroll into the setting sun with her ancestor.

Finally stopping, Ann stooped to pick up a ladybug and inquired if, in Emma's experience, she had learned the legend of ladybugs and the promise of good luck they carried? Emma timidly hunched her shoulders up.

"Farmers appreciate ladybugs because they help keep crops safe by eating other bugs that can damage what grows. But children share a secret about them," she added conspiratorially. "If a ladybug lands on you, you count the spots, and that's how many wishes you have."

Ann extended her hand, holding the tiny bug in her palm. She watched as it fluttered from her palm to Emma's shoulder. "Well, gracious me, Emma. It appears you have some wishes coming".

Emma stretched out her arm and watched in fascination as the bug traversed down her sun-streaked arm. She carefully lifted the ladybug, placing it in the center of her palm. She counted seven spots.

"What do you fancy, Emma"?

Ann waited for Emma to wish to journey home and was momentarily thrown off guard when the young girl responded passionately,

"I wish I could be a great dancer. I take dance lessons, but I'm not as good as the other girls."

Ann pondered the response and led Emma to a stout pine log inviting her to sit. The air was still, and Emma could no longer distinguish nature's sounds. The tiny, prickly hairs on her arms tingled. Ann gazed at the Sankofa carving resting in the palm of her hand. She raised it toward the sky and brandished her arms. To Emma's astonishment, an image of people from all walks of life appeared. There were doctors, lawyers, teachers, artists, and a dancer.

"Who are they?" Emma asked.

"They are ancestors and kinfolk. Some are rising generations; some are your descendants."

Ann's arm swayed once more in the breeze, and the vision shifted to an ancient African village teeming with life and bustling activity.

"The man sitting among the villagers is called a griot or storyteller. He is honored among the people because he preserves the history and culture of the tribe. He passes it down by reciting the village's stories to the next generation until a new griot is named. Sons and daughters were abducted and sold into slavery. Dismantling families corrupted the tradition of passing the torch of the Griot. The stolen had no one to tell them the stories of Africa and the ancestors."

Ann flung her arm again, and the image dissolved and morphed before her eyes. Emma recoiled at the appearance of enslaved men, women, and children working on a plantation. A boy cried and reached frantically for his mother as he was taken and forced into a wagon. His bare-footed mother ran behind the wagon until she could no longer keep up.

"Our people tried to hold on to their customs and history. But the corrupt abomination of slavery slanted our understanding of our origin. We nearly forgot who we were and from where we came. Our proper knowledge of selves was on the brink of extinction. Our ancestors were bought and sold without consideration of their culture.

"Nevertheless, there were still elders and storytellers. The colored preachers and teachers took on the job of the Griot. Some folks shared stories through song and dance, not just by word of mouth.

"We tell stories in present times, but we are always chasing the missing pieces. Some fragments lay uncelebrated at the bottom of the restless ocean, throughout the South, unmarked graves of the broken-hearted hold other bits. The truth is, we all play a role in preserving the chronicles of the elders. We pass the richness of our tales on to the next generation.

Would it surprise you to think of your mother as a griot writing the memoirs of her heritage? Annie tells stories with her splendid drawings. The Unknown summoned them to understand the importance of using their gifts to tell our story. Similarly, they have called you, Emma. One day, in your way, with your divine talents, you, too, will share a tale about our people.

"Throughout our history as a people in this country, we have been told what we could not do. The spirit of the Unknown Ancestor fills us with visions of what is possible. But it's only achievable if we have the heart and soul to imagine the marvels of the universe and believe. Most times, we must try harder, work smarter, do better, make more extraordinary efforts, but we can achieve almost anything. We all have doubts and fears, but we cannot surrender to that, least it robs us of our dreams."

Nodding, Ann offered the Sankofa carving to Emma, who hesitated initially, then decisively accepted the bird and waved the chiseled sculpture through the air. The vivid image of ancestors and family members materialized once more. Rising slowly from the log, Emma scrutinized the impressions deeper, moving from one person to another, perusing the sea of faces. She heard an ardent buzz of voices. Eyes squinting, her expression relaxed, and her lips curled up in recognition.

She spotted an adolescent with smooth and exquisite brown skin, one leg curled around the other, reading a book. *Gramby still sits with her legs tucked when she reads.* Emma's eyes bulged at her Aunt Lizzy's curly head bent over a textbook. It was her first year of medical school. Random posters and illustrations plastered the walls of Lizzy's small apartment. In the future, she would become a collector and become the first to plan an outing to a new exhibit in town. One of the reasons she and Annie connected.

Emma brightened at her mother's girlish blush strolling hand-in-hand with her dad on the campus of Howard University. The yard bustled with students, but her parents only had eyes for one another. People continued to parade by in the enchanting cinema in the sky. Emma recognized faces from dated photo albums. She wasn't familiar with all their names but was confident they were family.

Ultimately, Emma's impassioned gaze rested on the dancer. The prima ballerina floated with athleticism and grace. Her spins pierced the stratosphere with the intensity of a tornado, ending with a gazelle's refinement. It was only after the young woman landed the perfect grand jeté and struggled to contain the involuntary twitch of a grin threatening the corners of her mouth that it hit her. Emma was gazing at her future.

Ann interrupted Emma's musing, once again taking her hand. "You can do anything if you have the heart and soul to trust your instincts and believe. But for now, it's the sun will soon set, and time for us to rejoin the others. What about the rest of your wishes?"

Emma's cheeks warmed. "I think I will save them for later. I might need them while I'm here."

The young girl and older woman laughed in unison as they emerged through the fog. Eying her sister and the others, Emma ran, twirling and leaping gleefully towards them. The others eyeballed her, amazed, trying to comprehend what had happened during the stroll to bring about such a change in mood.

Emma finally stopped and confidently sauntered toward them. "Why are you all staring? Haven't you ever had the privilege of being in the presence of a prima ballerina?"

Placing one hand on her hip, Emma dramatically extended her arm, extending the wooden Sankofa carving toward the fading horizon. A ladybug landed on the carving. Carefully removing the ladybug, she swept the hand holding the bird slowly across the sky, and a vision emerged.

Cocking her head to the side, Emma proclaimed, "Someone has wishes coming today."

Five Mighty Anchors

"Missouri, a ladybug landed on your hand. Are you going to count those spots and discover how many wishes she sends your way? I bet you can wish for something extra special today."

Missouri cupped the tiny bug between her hands, silently counting the spots.

"Claudie, if I wished for anything more, the Lord might think me ungrateful for all He's already done for me. Don't misunderstand me now; it's not that I haven't had my share of sorrows that I wouldn't wish away. Lord knows there's plenty I could yearn for when it comes to my children and grandbabies too. But I am genuinely grateful for my blessings.

Trials and troubles are part of the time we spend on Earth. But my life came closer than most colored people to being just right.

I've lived a life I would have never imagined fifty years ago when I married Sweetie. Blessed with nine healthy children who attended school and came of age, that is something for these times. My brothers and sisters never considered college a possibility, but four of mine had the opportunity. I never had to worry about feeding my babies, even during the depression, and I have treasured memories and stories that will last through generations.

"Old Miss Gertie from church used to say, 'a son is the anchor of a mother's life.' Well, I had five mighty anchors. Early Lee, Aquilla, Ernest, Noah, and Emory. Each one is different, but a fraction of my heart making it whole right along with my daughters. Mine is a humble heart overflowing with pride.

When I imagine the tragedies that befell other families and what could have gone wrong but didn't? Well, I know it was more than just ladybug luck. Early, Aquilla, and Noah were all drafted during World War I, but only Early was stationed in Europe and fought. And blessed be, he came home safe. Those young men are my anchors and my pride and joy, and I could speak on each one all day.

My daughters too, mind you. I wouldn't want you or anyone to think I favored the boys over the girls. On the contrary, my daughters are a source of great joy, and their strength and courage are an inspiration to the next generation. But the mother and son bond is exceptional."

"Missouri, your face lights up as bright as the sun when you speak of your children."

Missouri's tone shifted as she searched Claudia's eyes. There was no sign of bitterness or anguish. "If I were to wish for anything, it would be for a different outcome for your sister. It grieves me to discuss Lilly and Aquilla, especially with you. A kind and gentle heart beats inside of you, Claudie Hogens, and I am fortunate to have you as a friend. You never let how Partner wronged Lilly spoil our friendship.

I can't remember how it came to be that people started calling Aquilla Partner, but he was not a fair partner to his wife. I have always regretted Partner placing Lilly in the sanitarium in Milledgeville, and I will be forever sorry Partner did not bring her home.

The government changed the dreadful name of that place from the Georgia State Lunatic, Idiot, and Epileptic Asylum to Central State Hospital, but switching the name didn't alter the conditions of that institution. They labeled Milledgeville the City of Crazies, and the treatment was frightful. They placed patients in hot and cold showers and straitjackets. The keepers locked children in metal cages.

Sweetie and I didn't intend for Mamie to stay there after Boots was born. We would have nothing to do with that institution.

Sweetie confronted Rank and put his foot down. For better or worse, Sweetie said, in sickness and in health, he demanded Rank bring Mamie home. Sweetie and Rank manage fine now, but it took a while for Sweetie to forgive Rank for taking Mamie there. I wasn't as angry with Rank at the time. The best of men make poor choices in troubled circumstances. He didn't have any idea what to do.

I understand there will always be unpleasant sentiments towards Sweetie for not stepping in for Lilly the way he did for Mamie. Joshua stood firm in his right to intervene because Mamie was his daughter. He believed Mr. Jake should have done the same for Lilly."

Reaching out to her dearest friend, Missouri wrapped Claudia's hands in hers, pulling them to her breasts. "My grandchildren resent Sweetie, as do other members of your family for not interceding and making Aquilla bring their mama home. I accept that and believe that to be a fair judgment. I'm so sorry, Claudie. If I supposed lady-bug wishes had a magic power, I would wish we could go back in time. My family would do better by Lilly and the children."

Pulling her hand back, Claudia swiped a tear away. "As you said, Missouri, life has its sorrows, and both our families have suffered. But today is not the day to dwell on the sadness. I want to hear more about those mighty anchors, as you call them. I was witness to them growing up, but they've done a heap of deeds through the years."

Exhaling, Missouri continued as reflections of the past drifted back to her sons.

"Noah passed on seven years ago at the age of thirty-six. He relocated to Chicago, thinking colored folks were doing better out there. Consumption was terrible, spreading all over the country, and Noah fell sick. He came home but never fully recovered. Livonia was a good wife. She cared for him until the end, and presently she does a good job making ends meet doing domestic work for white people. I help with the kids when I can. Nothing grieves a mother more than burying a child, even a grown one. I miss him every day.

"Aquilla's story is Sister Lilly's story as well. He married Lilly; you are wiser than most on how she became unbalanced, and Partner placed her in the institution for the demented. I am ashamed he has another Lilly now that he calls his wife when Lilly Calhoun is his wife in the eyes of God and the law. He works hard, farming some. He got that from Sweetie, and he's good at it. And he sells lumber all over Macon and makes a good living."

Missouri paused, studying Claudie to gauge her reaction. Sensing she was on solid ground with the conversation, she continued. "Sweetie is a God-fearing man. He doesn't take kindly to what he did or to Partner's secondary doings. He considers it the devil's work."

"Ernest is most like his father, stern and uncompromising. His calling to preach came before he enrolled in divinity school. The formal training gave him confidence, though the others aren't so sure it didn't make him self-righteous. He does hold sway over Lizzie Chapel the same way Sweetie holds power over the land and those sharecroppers. I'm proud of him, though. Not many preachers in these parts have two churches. He goes back and forth between Macedonia and Lizzie Chapel, and he has a good assistant pastor who helps him out.

"There is tension growing between him and Partner. Ernest disapproves of Aquilla calling the second Lilly his wife while still legally married to your sister. And don't let me start about the moonshine. Partner considers me too sheltered to be aware of that bootleg whiskey he keeps in the bottom of his wagon. I have it on good information that he sells it when he peddles wood. If the police pick him up, he will end up on Troy Raines' chain gang for sure, if not worse.

The rumors have reached Ernest and have tongues wagging. He has threatened to expel his brother from the church. And not just Aquilla, but his daughter, Missouri, as well. She is the only grandchild named for me. Missouri is planning on setting up a juke joint in the country. For sure, that will not turn out well. Partner says he's not waiting for Ernest to put him out of Lizzy Chapel. He's starting to attend service over at Unionville Baptist Church. Bad blood between brothers is never a good thing."

Missouri gazed again at the ladybug, flicking it away. "Ernest and his wife Lula never had children of their own, but God provided differently. My Gertrude married Lula's brother, Tom Gates. Some say the Gates are the most prosperous colored folks in these parts. That store of theirs has gas pumps, and even white folk obtain their service. Troy Raines is his main competition, but Gates holds his own even though Raines is white. Raines doesn't worry much about Gaines since he makes plenty of money running the chain gang."

"Gates thinks his money allows him to do what he wants, but money doesn't buy you character." Missouri was surprised Claudia offered an opinion of Tom Gates but didn't mention it

"Gertrude wailed in church every Sunday. Most folks assumed there were problems; they just were not aware of how bad. Tom Gates is a scoundrel, womanizing and tearing that family apart. Gertrude finally up and left him and her babies behind and hightailed it to Chicago. Ernest and Lula are raising their kids. I can't say I approve of her bailing out on her babies, but she stood as much as she could, and Lula and Ernest are devoted to those children.

And, of course, finally, there is my youngest anchor, Dr. Emory Martin Calhoun." Missouri crowed. "The others contend I spoil him, but he is the baby after all. I was so proud when he went off to college at Morehouse in Atlanta and then on to dental school at Meharry College of Medicine in Nashville, Tennessee."

"Everyone knows Doc," interjected Claudia, "the first colored dentist in Macon, Georgia."

"That almost didn't happen. When Emory graduated, he and all the colored men graduating from medical and dental school had to register in-person to take the license examination. That was so white folks could mark the applications and make sure most failed. So, always the prankster, Doc outsmarted them. Emory asked a white boy to sign up for him so he would sit for the test without them identifying him in advance and having his application marked. He passed with high scores and shocked those folk when they called his name, and a Negro walked onstage to collect his license."

Both women buckled with laughter.

Chapter 14

The Chain Gang

*I*n this peculiar land, each generation of Blacks faces its own appalling tribulation. Accordingly, slavery is legally abolished, but the battle for freedom and dignity persists. Humans who lack human empathy consistently scar my people, shifting them from the chains of slavery to the shackles of road gangs. There is a defect in these people driving them to the foul exploitation of Black souls.

As the United States settles into the twentieth century, the South struggles for economic parity, but its dilapidated roads block the conduits of commerce necessary for progress. Alarmed that advancement will bypass the southern region, its leading citizens turn to the system that produced its former prosperity, profiteering from others' cheap and free labor.

The rise of the prison system follows, and the "Good Roads Movement" spreads across the county. It begins with convict leasing, which fails to yield the desired effect of promoting Southern progress. Convict leasing hires out workers to private enterprises, including mills and farms. The competition for labor among business interests is fierce. More importantly, the government does not utilize the workforce to promote public interests.

People are vexed by the practice and push for an alternative. Georgia abolishes convict leasing in 1908 and, in due time leads the South in the *establishment and proliferation of the chain gang, a system of state-sponsored slavery and barbarism.*

The casualties of this revised criminal justice system are predominantly Black, and their crimes are misdemeanors. Poverty ensures they are unable to pay the fines imposed for their transgressions. The act of loitering is labeled a crime; purloining an apple is a breach of law and order. Drunkenness, fighting, even throwing rocks can plant a person in prison for thirty days or up to a year. It may have the hallmark of a short sentence, but the conditions on the chain gang can develop into a death sentence.

The punishment is brutal once the system swallows a person into its dark recesses. The overseers of slavery are now the bosses of the chain gangs. The foremen carry guns and whips studded with nails. They argue, "You can't get good work from a colored unless you beat em."

The judicial system excuses the cruelty of the gangs by accusing Blacks of possessing natural criminal tendencies.

They insist the system teaches a work ethic with the road gangs' forced labor and maintain the victims breath fresh air as they labor. Besides, they say, there is no point in paying Black people because they cannot handle money responsibly and spend it on liquor and deviant behavior. "Bad boys make good roads," or so the saying goes.

The conditions under which these men, women, and children labor are contemptible. They work from the sun's rising until it sinks in the western sky. The blistering rays strike the backs of the workers with nearly the same ferocity as the generously used whip or shovel. And when there is no sun, the grinding work of breaking rocks, digging ditches, and paving roads does not stop. When it rains, the drudgery endures.

The superiors transport five individuals united by iron ankle chains called hobbles to work sites crammed side by side in converted railroad cars. The chains do not come off when the prisoners work, sleep, or relieve themselves. They are always tethered to one another. They shuffle along as passersby throw objects at them, deride the battered souls with laughter, and hurl spit upon them until they reach the worksite. Their food is rotten with maggots. There is no bathing or bedding. The weight of the chains causes sores and infections. There is no medical treatment. Any minor infraction of the rules results in a beating or time jammed in the wooden sweatbox with a corrugated metal roof. No one can say with certainty how many prisoners died on the chain gang.

Be it the mercy of the gods or the guardianship of the Unknown ancestors, the valiant descendants demonstrate again they are resilient survivors; some are old, some young, all of them destined for calamity even in the bosom of survival.

Chapter 15

Lizella

The four youngsters listened with rapt attention as Missouri and Claudia reminisced on the unconventionality of life in Lizella, Georgia. The long-worn family tales relayed in vibrant first-person encounters validated their place in storied family genealogy and breathed life into archaic memorials. The Early Calhoun Missouri spoke of lovingly was the resolute young soldier who fought for his country in World War I. Aunt Gertrude was a conflicted young mother in an abusive marriage who believed her only choice was to run to escape her misery. Doc, the youngest, would be forever remembered as the prankster dentist with a sense of humor who made everyone laugh. Missouri was the nucleus of it all.

"Everyone in our time refers to Joshua as the backbone of the family. Missouri had as much to do with her children's success as he did. Maybe more," declared Annie. "She mediated family disputes to keep the peace and supported the dreams and aspirations of her children, nieces, nephews, and friends. Missouri McElmurry Calhoun carried the same resilience and determination the Unknown Ancestor possessed to survive the Middle Passage. My upcoming art exhibit highlights the history of the McElmurry and Calhoun family. I will make it my goal to ensure Missouri receives as much esteem as

Joshua. Actually, all our women ancestors deserve more admiration and appreciation than they receive".

Annie removed the sketchbook from her knapsack and started to draw the two women while they talked of days gone by. She launched a reformed version of the ancestor who had not been sufficiently honored.

Her story captured much more than simply two individuals talking. Annie artistically narrated the tale of a deep abiding friendship and sincere affection between women who had experienced life in divergent ways. Trust and companionship united a pair of friends, one of means the other with scant possessions, yet both understood they were survivors of a nation that valued neither of them.

Annie sketched while the others gazed, mesmerized by images of a mystical glimpse into the past, or more accurately, the future. Engrossed with Missouri's chronicles, they relished the scene as if watching a movie screen in the sky. The spectacle was suddenly interrupted by bells tolling loudly, scattering the ghostly visions and startling them from their reverie.

Vesper gongs pealed from multiple directions. Ann explained how the landowners rang bells to signal to the sharecroppers in the field that it was time to wrap up the workday. Joshua Calhoun's bell was the loudest, and most field hands listened for it no matter for whom they worked. If Joshua's workers could leave, it was safe to say everyone could quit for the day and go home because his bell was never early, but it was always on time.

"And that's our signal to head home as well," said Ann.

The group gathered their things, following Ann to the clay-packed road. It was pointless to ask where they were going or what would happen next. They understood that whatever path they traveled, an adventure awaited them. Besides, asking questions in advance never got them answers anyway.

The overabundance of noise penetrating Jay's senses was eerie, but he was growing accustomed to listening and distinguishing what lurked about and who might cause them harm. The others were unaware of the clanging, but Jay caught the mournful sound before any of the others. Soon they all took note of the clatter, even before the detainees materialized.

The rattling of the chains grew louder, broadcasting the approach of chain-gang prisoners. The disturbance communicated perilous though unfamiliar circumstances to the young transplants from the twenty-first century.

A man on horseback came into view, preceding the prisoners. The rider lacked emotion. The spent animal appeared as weary as those he led, kicking up a low cloud of dust in front of the group of down-trodden men shuffling behind. Dressed in grey striped uniforms, they reeked of a foul body odor, a combined scent of sweat, human waste, and Georgia clay. They were weak and exhausted. Men brandishing whips and guns moved alongside them, yelling commands and obscenities, the convicts managed to ignore. The man in charge was perched in a wagon, pulling up the rear. A pretentious Troy Raines, head of the county chain gang system, sat ostensibly oblivious to the torture he controlled; or presumably taking pride in his power.

Dread swept the group as they recognized the man they encountered on the street earlier that day. Raines's expression gnarled as he menacingly inspected Jay, who took an unconscious step back, trying in vain to shake the fear the man's hostile frown stirred in him.

The youngsters passed the prisoners, cautious not to stare, and continued for another mile until they reached a large piece of property that included a spacious farmhouse with a covered porch and stately pillars.

Annie immediately recognized the house. "This is Joshua and Missouri's place. My sister will give you supper, and you will spend the night here."

Joshua Calhoun sat on the porch reading the newspaper, and if he took notice of the new arrivals, his demeanor demonstrated no such evidence. Missouri stepped through the door smiling at the children as she and Ann exchanged perceptive glances.

The group of prisoners eventually caught up and kept moving forward, but Troy Raines stopped his wagon, jumped down, and climbed the steps to the porch where Joshua Calhoun sat, taking a seat in a nearby rocking chair.

An unconventional association existed between the two men, and every evening, Raines made a habit of stopping by Joshua's homestead for a visit. Of course, Joshua never invited him in, nor would he have accepted had the offer been made. One would not describe the relationship as a friendship; no such bonds existed between a white and Black man in Georgia during that time. Missouri assumed Raines viewed Joshua as a curiosity and was determined to discover how a colored man came to be so smart.

"Evening, Joshua."

Meticulous in his ability to show no emotion, Joshua's dispassionate eyes shifted slightly towards the prisoners.

"Evening, Troy."

"I passed your fields. It seems that you're going to have a good year if the weather continues to cooperate, observed Raines."

"I reckon," Joshua answered.

Joshua paused before centering his full attention on the prisoners then back to Raines. "My fields may look fine, but them boys don't appear to be holding up too good, Troy. Can't figure out how you rouse out the work you need to be done from them when they're weak and hungry."

If Raines was disturbed by Joshua's criticism, he didn't show it.

"They're all right, 'cept that one in the back. He's the laziest boy I've ever had. I swear, Joshua, I think I'm going to have to kill him; too much effort to feed him and scrape so little work out of him."

Nearby, Annie flinched, listening to Raines's heartless words. The young boy, who could not have been much older than she, was gaunt and covered in dust. His eyes were sunken, and his despair assaulted Annie's sense of justice. Filled with compassion, she feared for the boy's safety. Would Raines really kill him? His tone suggested he was not beyond such a cold-blooded act.

Missouri came through the door with a tray of lemonade, disturbed to find Annie listening intently to the conversation between the two men. She was also aware of Raines paying too much attention to the children, especially Jay. Smiling sweetly at Raines, she moved down the steps towards Annie after serving him. "Baby, go round back and help take down that laundry. The rest of you go on and wash up for supper."

As he continued to gaze at Jay, Raines could not contain his curiosity and asked Joshua if they were his grandchildren. Joshua brushed off the question with a comment about having too many grandchildren to count or to pay them much attention.

The men continued their visit as the Calhoun household settled into its evening customs. Family members milled about as boys brought in wood, and girls set the table and folded laundry. Annie, Josh, Emma, and Jay joined in with the household routine, and if anyone were curious about their presence, none would have the temerity to question Missouri in her home. As they helped finish the minor chores and prepared to eat, Annie summoned the courage to ask Missouri how Mr. Joshua, as she thought best to call him, could be friends with a man as mean as Troy Raines.

Wiping her hands on her apron, Missouri exhaled and scrutinized Annie. "I'm not sure I would call what Sweetie and Troy Raines have a friendship. The Bible says God causes His sun to rise on the evil and the good and sends rain on the righteous and the unrighteous just the same. Sweetie keeps his eye on Troy Raines for survival, Baby. We always try to be mindful of what them folk are up to. Sometimes, having an association with them comes in right handy."

Later, as they prepared to eat, Missouri picked up her Bible and read from Jeremiah Chapter 29 verse 7. "It says here, *Also, seek the peace and prosperity of the city to which I have carried you into exile. Pray to the Lord for it because if it prospers, you too will prosper.*"

She carefully closed the Bible, her appraising eyes directed towards Annie. "We did not choose this place as our home, but this here is our land, and we intend for it to prosper so that we, too, will thrive. Now Lord, bless this food we are about to eat."

At that moment, a young girl burst into the room. "Grandma, Aunt Mamie is in labor, and they say she got a bad fever. She's talking out her head, and they need you to come."

Chapter 16

Infirmities and Afflictions

Truth and integrity are the foundation of our story. Without them, the descendants will never appreciate the resilience of their ancestors. So, I confess possessing the knowledge that belittling and abusing people with melanin in their skin started long before pirates and profiteers brought Blacks to the colonies. Dark skin has been equated with diminished value since humankind first observed differences in skin tones. Diminished value justifies one group's despicable deeds when dominating another.

People protect and nurture what they esteem. Our humanity was not the substance of our value to the colonizers and their descendants. Utilizing our gifts and supplying labor at no cost was our only worth to them. Thus, the view of superiority flourished in a fledgling nation partitioned by race and exploiting skin color to tyrannize a people for economic gain. It was not surprising that brutal domination emerged, though perhaps those who designed the system invested too much hope in believing it would be unsustainable for generations.

Primacy is and always has been about power. What better way to exert control over oppressed people than to minimize their physical well-being? The presumed greatest thinkers of the world ratified the notion that men and women of color were inferior, thus affirming the worthlessness of the enslaved. Theoretical inferiority justified the institution of chattel slavery and the overall neglect of the health and welfare of the enslaved. The political leadership integrated substandard treatment of those in bondage into laws of the land.

Lamentably, freedom did not change the persistence of insufficient care and opportunity. Throughout the land, it was common practice to deny primary care and services to Black people. Hospitals and health facilities were rarities for colored folks, for sure in the South and elsewhere. When white providers treated our people, it was, with few reservations, through indifferent and bigoted eyes. In the worse cases, researchers used Blacks as guinea pigs for experimentation.

With minimal exceptions, the Howard University School of Medicine and Meharry Medical College were the sole sources of trained Black medical and health professionals for more than half of the twentieth century. Even with training, Black doctors were denied hospital privileges in most facilities. Black healthcare in the early part of the century was rarely administered in a hospital or by anyone with medical training. Life-saving medicine was unavailable or too expensive to be wasted on colored people.

Still, we managed to care for ourselves with remedies and treatments passed down from the healers and shamans. The old mothers treated all nature of illnesses. The midwives delivered babies and reared children to be healthy and hard-working women and men. When the old mothers could not bring the children into the world in good health, families cared for them until the Almighty consumed their last breaths, young and old.

Undoubtedly, there were defeats and losses; and outsiders blamed the healers for their backward social customs, ignorance, and inferior treatments. The medical groups detailed a litany of Negro diseases better left untreated. Consumption and syphilis were the leading killers in the 1920s. Giving birth was life-threatening for all women.

The descendants of colonizers spoke of Darwin and the survival of the fittest. Ironically, few species could have survived the tribulations faced by our people from the moment the first boat left the shores of Africa. But my folk withstood unimaginable maltreatment and afflictions and still survived. This mighty race survived all manner of infirmities and afflictions.

Chapter 17

All Alone

Annie followed Missouri out of the house, praying the family matriarch would not force her to turn back. Missouri rushed along the clay-packed road, her grim expression mimicking the terror churning in the pit of Annie's stomach. The blissful hope of the spring evening was in stark contrast to the dread swirling around Missouri. The usual attention of Annie's artistic eye failed to appreciate the explosive colors and sweet fragrance of the hyacinths along the way.

Unable to pace her stride to move quickly enough, Missouri began to run, surprising Annie at how swiftly the older woman could move. Annie picked up her tempo to match Missouri's determined sprint.

It was irrational to be scared. Annie was well aware Mamie had seven children, and this baby was the fourth. She would survive this arduous labor and go on to have three more children, but that awareness didn't calm Annie's fears.

Annie's aunt Lizzy was an obstetrician and talked about women giving birth, sharing stories about complicated deliveries. Modern medicine and highly trained doctors of Lizzy's caliber resolved most unanticipated difficulties. But this was 1923 in rural Georgia, and Mamie was Black. Annie was smart enough to understand Mamie was facing was an uphill battle, and this delivery was more than merely complicated. She searched her memory for accounts of Mamie having medical problems. There was talk of Mamie's gentle spirit and plain conversational style, but that wasn't that just a sign of the times?

The two ran until they arrived at a simple house on the edge of the Calhoun property. They reached Mamie and Rank's home just as Joshua drove past in the farm's old Model T truck. Annie wondered why he would leave during a time of crisis, but his expression was determined, and clearly, he had a purpose and a destination in mind. She hoped he was going for help. Mamie's husband Rank stood alone in the yard; a helpless expression absorbed his face.

Alena Webb Jones, a midwife and Rank's mother, greeted Missouri and Annie at the door. Her native heritage was evident. She was a Cherokee daughter with high cheekbones who twisted her long hair in braids. Over the years, she'd learned to merge the herbal medicines of her native people with the remedies she learned from the Black shaman after her marriage to Thomas Jones. She was the most prominent healer in the area, but she was no miracle worker.

"It's been hours," she said solemnly to Missouri, "and I can't do nothing to hasten that baby or break Mamie's fever."

The women entered the small house while Rank remained outside. Gazing around the house, Annie was reminded of Fox's 1867 cabin, though this one was smaller. Its tiny parlor with a wood-burning stove and two bedrooms off the side was sparsely furnished. Two rocking chairs and a wooden table with benches on either side dominated the room. The room was stifling with no circulation of air.

Notably missing was the bustle and warmth of family fellowship common to the McElmurry-Calhoun clan. Childbirth was serious and dangerous. The fewer people around, the better. Darkness enveloped the room as Lena had followed the tradition of covering the windows with blankets during birthing. A pot boiled on the stove, and a pungent scent unfamiliar to Annie floated in the atmosphere.

Annie's reflections on her surroundings were interrupted by a piercing scream from one of the two rooms. Mamie's wail vibrated throughout the small space, momentarily breaking the women's low-pitched tones. Annie ventured to the opening of one of the back rooms and dared to approach Mamie's bedside. She had never witnessed anyone in labor as she absorbed the scene and the writhing woman, drenched in sweat, destined to be her great-great-grandmother.

"It's me, Annie," she whispered as she neared the old wrought iron bed containing two mattresses. "This baby is a girl, and she will be my great-grandmother. You are destined to be the mother of seven children. This little one is number four. In the future, I had a vision of you at a party celebrating your parents' fiftieth wedding anniversary. You were smiling and enjoying your family. You will survive this and be alright."

Indifferent to Annie's presence, Mamie murmured and babbled words and phrases that made zero sense to Annie. Mamie rocked and cradled her bulging stomach in endless agony. Her tortured expression strained the muscles in her face, and terror was in her eyes.

Lena pushed Annie aside as Mamie began to moan louder at the onset of another contraction. Wrapping her arm around Mamie's shoulder, Lena held a bowl under her nose with the liquid from the boiling pot. Mama thrashed, and Annie was sure she would knock the bowl from Lena's hands.

Annie backed away and asked Missouri a question, although she already anticipated the response.

"Can't we take her to a hospital?"

Missouri shook her head. "The hospitals here don't accept colored people."

Nearly three hours passed before Joshua arrived, accompanied by a stout white man carrying a battered medical case. A dazed Missouri greeted Dr. Applewhite, who had once saved another of her children. Years earlier, she and Josh met the doctor when their youngest child Lilla was treated for consumption at the state sanitarium in Alto, Georgia. A groundbreaking facility in public health, Alto was Georgia's most ambitious health project, and it was considered one of the most progressive facilities in the nation. The medical community commended the sanitarium for its innovative treatment of tuberculosis.

What's more, to the surprise of many, its construction included a wing for colored patients. Lilla Calhoun was treated in the colored branch of Alto and survived tuberculosis when many others throughout the South perished. Dr. Applewhite was responsible for saving her life. Furthermore, he had gone beyond treating Lilla; he had shown Missouri and Joshua respect when they visited their daughter and explained Lilla's care and treatment to them.

Joshua and Missouri were thankful for the care Lilla received at the time and were indebted to this doctor for his dedication to the practice of medicine and his willingness to place humanity over skin color. And while he had demonstrated enormous compassion during Lilla's illness, coming to Mamie's home was extraordinary. Missouri could not imagine what Josh had said or done to convince him to come all this way for Mamie. But a lifetime of experience had taught her; Sweetie always had his methods. Missouri and Lena stepped aside to allow the doctor to examine Mamie.

After assessing Mamie's condition, Dr. Applewhite stepped away from the bed and despondently told the small group there was not much he could do for Mamie at this point. He explained that nature would take its course, and hopefully, the baby would survive. But Mamie's fever had probably persisted for too long. She would probably be blind if she lived, or her mind would be impaired.

"You mean she be crazy?" asked Lena.

"We prefer not to use that word, but there could be damage. It's also possible mother and child will both die. I'm sorry."

"They won't die," Annie pronounced emphatically. "I'm proof they won't die."

"Hush child," Missouri snapped.

Since her arrival, Josh focused his deep-set eyes on Annie for the first time. Gazing at Missouri, he shook his head slightly and muttered, "Bedeviled McElmurrys."

Late in the night, Mamie gave birth to her fourth child, a healthy baby girl mockingly named Alone. Ill-fated Mamie continued to burn with what Lena referred to as childbed fever. When the fever finally broke, a listless Mamie lay blankly staring into the distance. Annie again crept to Mamie's bedside. Tears stained her cheeks as she slipped the Sankofa carving into Mamie's hand, squeezing it between her slender fingers. She wished with all her might to return with

Mamie to the period before her labor began. Perhaps help would be available before it was too late.

Annie's shoulders sagged as she dropped her head on the side of the bed. Missouri stroked her hair. The tender touch of Missouri's hand reached the depths of her soul. Unable to contain her emotions any longer, Annie sobbed and grieved for the wit and insight lost in her great-great-grandmother's spirit. 'Missouri tried handing the baby to Mamie. She gave no evidence of maternal instinct or motherly experience despite having three other children. Whether it was exhaustion or indifference, Mamie was in an unreachable place. Finally, after speaking with Rank, Missouri decided it was best to bring the newborn baby to her home until Mamie regained her strength.

It was past sunrise when Joshua's car pulled into the yard of the Calhoun homestead carrying Missouri and the baby. Annie said in the bed of the truck, depleted of energy. The house bustled with activity. As Missouri prepared to place the child in a cradle she kept at the home, everyone fussed over the baby. A composed Emma was helping the girls make breakfast and lunch pails for the boys set to work in the fields.

Jay sauntered through the back of the house with an armload of wood. She wondered how he maintained his twenty-first-century swagger in that ridiculous 1923 outfit. He'd been a good sport about hurling through time. He had mentioned his interest in her more than once, and it was before all this began. Becoming better acquainted with him once they returned home was going to be another adventure. For the first time in hours, she was not overwhelmed by despair.

Not wanting any part of working in the fields, Josh gazed quizzically at Annie. "Are we done here yet"?

Annie sighed and eyed Josh affectionately.

"I screwed up Josh by not telling you and Emma everything that happened when we time traveled in July. I'm sorry. I promise if you don't remember our travels this time, I will tell you everything. Then, if you realize you might have to do fieldwork, you can opt not to come back with me again", Annie joked.

A faint hint of a smirk crossed Josh's face as his eyes rested on his cousin. "Mark this day in history. It is the first time you have ever apologized to me, Annie".

Reaching out, she drew him into a hug.

"Soon, Josh," she murmured, "we're going home very soon."

Throughout the morning, Annie helped Missouri around the house and with the new baby. Ann would be coming by anytime now, and she would explain how the Sankofa sculpture would transport them to the anniversary party and then home. Annie did a quick sketch of Alone and considered how her mother would react upon hearing she had held Sophie's grandmother in her arms.

The noon lunch bell began tolling when Joshua burst into the house.

Alarmed by the prospect of more bad news, Missouri and Annie waited patiently as Joshua paced back and forth. At long last, he stopped and glared at Missouri. In a low menacing tone, he repeated several times, "for better or worse, in sickness and in health. That is what he promised before God, and that's how he will have her."

Missouri dared not speak and waited patiently to uncover what had upset her husband.

Eventually, he stopped pacing and spit out the word "Milledgeville."

Missouri gasped as her hand sprung to her mouth in horror. Joshua Calhoun's words were slow and measured, never mentioning his son-in-law's name.

"He committed my daughter to Milledgeville, an insane asylum, because she got sick giving birth to his daughter. Grabbing his shotgun, he headed for the door. "He will go back and bring her home, or I will kill him."

Chapter 18

Captured

Annie rushed to the covered porch appraising Joshua's resolve to take the life of his son-in-law as he drove away. A preposterous image of the antique Ford burning rubber and speeding towards Rank and Mamie's house popped into her head. But the car chugged along, giving Annie an idea. The old car was faster than a buggy but still slow by Annie's standards, and she made the rash decision to follow her ancestor.

Convinced she could stop Joshua before he did something he would later regret, Annie skipped down the broad steps and began running after the car. The brown and bulky woolen skirt and awkward lace-up shoes she wore were a far cry from proper running clothes, but she had a natural speed to her advantage, and she recalled the route Missouri followed the previous day that would hasten her brief trip to Mamie's.

Pausing for a moment to survey her surroundings, she pivoted race across the field where the laundry hung, increasing the odds of reaching Mamie's house in the shortest amount of time. Gathering the skirt in her hands, she took off again. It was an implausible chase but worth the effort to Annie.

Jay stepped from behind the gleaming white sheets, blowing in the April breeze, blocking her path. Attempting to side-step him, they shimmied left and right in a graceless dance until he grabbed her shoulders. "You aren't here to change the past or fix things."

Annie launched into a protest but eventually dropped her head. Warm tears slipped down her cheeks as Jay enveloped her in a hug. At long last, the pent-up emotion she'd repressed since the birth of Alone the night before erupted. The tears morphed into uncontrollable sobs as she wept for Mamie and the injustice suffered by her ancestors. Annie cried, mindful that she was incapable of altering history, not just for Mamie but for everyone who'd suffered under this brutal racist system.

Jay waited patiently for Annie to regain her composure. Finally, she stepped back, sheepishly glancing up at Jay. "How did you find me? More to the point, what makes you believe I am trying to change the past."

"A voice told me to intercept you. It implied you were headed for trouble, not that warning you of imminent trouble would be enough to stop you from rushing ahead. Besides, after what happened to Mamie, I assumed you were out to alter what is not yours to transform."

With sparkling eyes, Jay blinked and bent towards her. Anticipating what was coming, a bloom of color flushed Annie's cheeks. It wasn't the middle school dance or her life in the twenty-first century. It wasn't how she imagined it would be, but in her great-great-great grandmother's field in Lizella, Georgia, in 1923, Annie Sesstry experienced her first kiss, and it was perfect.

"Joshua is going to kill Rank."

"No, he isn't. If that had happened, it would be legendary in your family history. Furthermore, you told me Mamie had seven children. Do you have reason to believe the last three were not Rank's children"?

"I wasn't prepared for Mamie's brain damage."

"Who said it was brain damage?"

Confused, Annie wondered why she'd said Mamie suffered brain damage during her labor if she had not known that previously.

"I remember someone mentioning a train ride from Georgia once and how odd it was that Mamie was able to distinguish Newark from New York when a cousin prepared to leave the train too soon. I can't recall the context, and I didn't pursue it because it didn't make sense. All anyone ever talked about was how Mamie was the first in the family to go to college and how much of a Renaissance man Joshua was because she was a girl, and he supported her education. I never asked my grandmother much about her."

"Well, now when you're back you can ask. But that would be a vital detail for the family scribes and historians to omit. Emma and Josh's memories were lost after their initial time travel. Maybe you've been blocking what you don't want to recall about Mamie. I find it hard to believe you never questioned your mother or grandmother more about her since she has been so pivotal in your quest. Why would your mother leave a matter so crucial out of your family story?

Maybe after your first meeting with her, you never viewed her in any other way but perfect, so you buried it. But no matter what happened to her last night, she came to you more than a hundred years after she was preparing for college, more than fifty years after she died. She's been guiding you and protecting you in your search for the Unknown Ancestor. The Unknown Ancestor, whoever they were, has been safeguarding the both of you. Take the win, Annie."

Grasping her hand, Jay pulled her along and started strolling down the path. Despite her giddy contentment, the blissful intimacy they enjoyed would soon be interrupted. Annie was so engrossed in her conversation with Jay; she failed to notice they were proceeding into a deepening wooded area that should have been familiar to her.

She disregarded the weathered trees with moss garnishing the trunks and the thickening brush and briar that would later prick the palm of her hand. A second glance might have prepared her as she was swept into the nightmares haunting her sleep over the past several weeks.

It wasn't until Jay stopped abruptly, and she followed his glance to the scraggly human form dangling from a branch, that her surroundings and the circumstances became immediately unmistakable. She wanted to believe that the emaciated figure with the hollow expression in his eyes was an effigy, but the brutal words uttered by Troy Raines rang in her ears. *He's the laziest boy I've ever had. I swear,*

Joshua, I think I'm going to have to kill him. She recognized the young boy hanging from the tree as the same one on the chain gang. The same boy, Troy Raines, told Joshua he might have to kill. Unable to contain her emotions, she let out a biting howl that reverberated through the trees. The piercing scream brought two men rushing from deeper in the wood. Troy Raines followed them.

"Catch them," barked Raines.

"Run, Annie!" shouted Jay.

Both youngsters sped off, with Jay pushing Annie in one direction while darting in another. She was wearing the lace-up boots and a high-necked blouse, the identical ones from her nightmare. How could she not have remembered these clothes? It should have been a warning. Now, identical to the dream scenario, her clothes were an obstacle to her movement. But this was not a dream, and she and Jay were in danger. The sound of the dogs barking, and Jay yelling shattered the atmosphere.

She turned, catching the toe of her boot on an exposed root, and grabbed for a thorn-covered branch that stabbed her palm. As she began to topple over, strong arms caught her and carried her out of the woods. Upon waking from her dreams, Annie assumed Fox saved her and brought her out of the woods. But as the sun shifted and the man sat her under the tree, she was startled to find Joshua Calhoun standing over her.

Rubbing her bloody hands on her skirt, Annie jumped to her feet, preparing to head back into the woods, but Joshua restrained her. Jerking loose and spinning on her heels, she readied herself to do battle with the older man.

"Where do you think you're going," asked Joshua.

"Your friend Troy Raines has my friend Jay, and I am going back to get him."

Joshua's laugh was sinister. "You reckon a little girl such as yourself can tackle Troy Raines and his men"?

"He killed a man."

"He's killed many men and women too, I speck, but he won't kill your friend. He'll just put him where that other boy was, and no one will be wiser. We all resemble one another to them people."

Annie's mouth dropped open. "Jay is not going to work on the chain gang. You can't let that happen."

"Why would I stop it"?

"He didn't do anything."

"Most of them boys didn't do anything; your friend ain't my problem."

"My grandmother told me her mother found you to be a cold and callous man, and she was right."

"I am not familiar with your grandma or her mama. Who exactly might they be"?

Joshua suspiciously studied the girl who stood before him. His wary expression halted Annie's words and prevented her from going any further in explaining their family connection. It was clear that time traveling was passed down through the McElmurrys, not the Calhouns. It was unclear how informed Joshua was or what he believed about his wife's family. He'd called the McElmurrys bedeviled when she announced that Mamie and Alone wouldn't die.

The older Anne mentioned Joshua was not keen on Missouri spending much time with her family. Could that be because he believed the McElmurrys were under some sort of spell? She'd said Joshua was a devout man who went to a different, more zealous church from Missouri and the McElmurrys. If Annie told him Alone was her great-great-grandmother, he might think her insane or, worse, a witch. What could she share that would galvanize him into a rescue attempt of Jay?

Nervous tension radiated between adult and teen. Annie concluded it was best not to tell him the truth or depend on Joshua to save Jay. She would devise a plan of her own to rescue him before something terrible happened. Until then, she needed a plan to throw Joshua off the scent of the McElmurrys unique talent.

Sticking out her chin, she said, "My grandma is a McElmurry and kin to Miss Claudia Hogan as well."

"Then maybe, you need to sashay back to Miss Claudia Hogan's house and stay away from my family."

Chapter 19

Sankofa Send Off

Annie made direct eye contact with Joshua Calhoun, conceding she would have to find a way to free Jay without his assistance. But if he eventually recalled the peculiar children he encountered in 1923, she wanted him to remember a loyal and unwavering young girl. Her McElmurry and Calhoun bloodline, coupled with the resilience of the Unknown Ancestor, could never allow her to abandon her friend.

Her encounter with him had been disheartening. Joshua possessed an emotional detachment to others' circumstances that Annie found difficult to tolerate.

Yet, if she was charitable, she could begrudgingly grant him a pass. She speculated his attitude resulted from the Southern experience of Black people in these times. Still, the indifference to the troubles of anyone outside his immediate circle made it difficult to have any fondness for this ancestor that everyone revered in her time.

Having given up any delusion he would assist in rescuing Jay, she faked acceptance of his mandate to return to her family without further measures. She calmly stated her intention to return to the house, inform Missouri, and express her thanks for the family's hospitality and kindness. She promised she would be heading home shortly. Annie politely voiced her appreciation for his assistance in the woods but stood firmly in her place, determined not to make the first move to leave. His tall frame and menacing stare would not intimidate her.

Shoulders back and head held high, Annie willed herself to remain still. Joshua In due course, Joshua began the trek to his car, stopping once to glance back at her. Had Annie not been so anxious, she might have caught the slight upturn of his mouth and the expression of pride in Josh's eyes.

Heaving a sigh of relief at her tiny victory, Annie jabbed her finger in the air and declared her determination to save Jay.

"I can do this without you," she shouted in the direction the old car headed.

The bolstered teen marched resolutely toward the house, fingering the carving in her pocket with one hand, scrunching the curls in her hair with the other, and uttering her concerns aloud to the Unknown Ancestor.

"OK wise one, it's time for some Sankofa voodoo or whatever it is that makes this time travel possible. We must leave this era. But first, we need to save Jay. It will require intercepting the chain gang and creeping close enough to Jay, so when we yell Sankofa, the four of us transport all at once. Please, let us shift times when we pronounce it. I'm convinced Fox's prayer added extra mojo. I only wish I could catch a glimpse of Troy Raines's ugly face when we disappear right in front of his eyes".

Detouring to the fields, she located Josh raking lanes of soil and signaled for him to join her. Josh was not sorry to store the farm tools and bid farewell to the backbreaking work forever. Annie paraded with resolve and searched for Emma when they arrived at the house. She breathed in the fruity aroma locating her sister in the kitchen peeling apples along with their cousins. Drawing her outside, they connected with Josh waiting on the porch. Plopping down on the steps, she hesitated briefly before telling them why she'd summoned them.

"It's time for us to leave, but first, we have to rescue Jay."

"Rescue Jay from what"? Asked Josh.

"The chain gang."

"The What?" exclaimed both kids in unison.

"It's a long story, and I will explain later, but right now, we need a plan."

In her haste to talk with Emma and Josh, Annie hadn't noticed the older Ann sitting at the far end of the porch resting on the wooden swing attached to the ceiling by heavy anchor rope. Ann's toes tenderly pushed the swing as she rocked baby Alone.

"Now, what have you youngins gone and gotten yourselves into this time?"

Annie exhaled.

"Troy Raines snatched Jay to replace the prisoner he killed from the chain gang, and we have to save Jay and vault back to our own time."

Ann nodded. She carefully stood, making her way over to where the threesome loitered on the steps. She stood swaying and cooing at the baby before gazing at them shaking her head. "So, you're gonna just mosey up to the chain gang, guarded by men with guns, and take your friend"?

"Is there a better idea"?

"No, I reckon not. But you will have to be very careful."

Thinking for a moment, Ann began to hatch a plan. "I presume you plan to snatch your friend when Troy Raines stops for iced tea or lemonade this evening. That will be the only occasion when the gang is not moving, and you will have a chance to distract him and the guards and help Jay escape."

"Exactly. The only problem is that it would require cooperation from Mr. Joshua, and he already said he would not help," said Annie.

"Pay no attention to Joshua. His actions speak louder than his words. Gather your things. I speck you will want to say goodbye to Mamie before you leave, though she won't have much to say back to you."

"Is she here?" asked an astonished Annie.

"Rank brought her here from Milledgeville after Joshua talked with him. She's resting in the back bedroom".

Ann bent her time-worn face toward the baby, kissing her tiny forehead. "She and this little angel will stay awhile so Missouri can take care of them until Mamie is better. Go on now and take Mamie a warm cup of tea. Then you will do exactly as I say."

Annie rushed into the house, stopping by the kitchen to prepare a cup of tea, then tiptoed to the room where Mamie lay resting on a large bed with an intricately carved head and footboard. Layers of cozy, gleaming white cotton sheets and a handmade patch quilt covered the bed. Awake, Mamie's head faced an open window embellished by eyelet-trimmed curtains billowing out into the afternoon breeze. Sunlight streamed through, and dust particles sparkled and floated on air.

If not for Mamie's condition, Annie could envision sitting in the window seat with a sketchbook, talking to Mamie, capturing the idyllic beauty of the room and the gentle spirit of the woman lying on the bed.

Annie made no effort to speak to Mamie. She set the tea down while fluffing the pillows as best she could without disturbing the fragile woman; then, she lifted the cup to Mamie's lips. Mamie's eyes were distant, faraway in a world that excluded Annie and her surroundings, though she sipped the tea offered to her, taking breaths as she drank. Annie set it aside when the cup was empty, picked up a brush from the dresser, and gently stroked Mamie's disheveled hair. At long last, whispering goodbye, Annie kissed the cheek of her great-great-grandmother. As she readied herself to step away from the bed, Mamie reached up and cupped Annie's face. Annie blinked back tears as Mamie peered deep into Annie's eyes and sighed.

Josh and Annie gathered their belongings along with Emma's and headed to the start of the road leading to the Calhoun homestead. It was the spot Ann told them to place and cover their things with brush. Annie was to wait for the group to come by. Ann reminded her to concentrate as hard as she could so Jay could listen to the words spoken in her head and anticipate his pending rescue. Emma would remain with Ann until it was time to play her role in the rescue plan.

Ann anticipated that Raines would come up to the porch just as he did every other day, and his men and the prisoners would wait until his daily visit with Joshua ended. Annie would hide close to the road but remain out of sight. Raines might recognize her even from a distance, and the two men who were with him earlier in the woods would undoubtedly be among the guards. They reviewed the plan multiple times until they were confident and secure in their responsibilities. Josh hugged Annie for luck and headed back to his holding position.

At last, the imposing melancholy toll of the Calhoun bell rang out, signaling the end of the workday. Each clapper strike inside the bell pounded against Annie's heart like a hammer slapping her chest. Her muscles tightened as she fought to control her breathing. The pungent sulfuric odor of the Georgia clay stung her nostrils as she inhaled the dust enveloping the weeds and grass around her. Gnats flew around her hair as she resisted the urge to stand up and smack every creepy, crawly thing invading her space. Her ears picked up the sound of the workers in the fields shutting down. How long, she wondered, would it be until Raines and his captives came dragging up the road.

The dissonance of the mobile jail was barely audible at first, but then the sound of the field-holler in the distance jolted Annie. There was no mistaking Jay's clear voice crying out the lead lines of the chant. Did he suspect their escape plan for him needed to place them nearby, and was them that he was on the way?

It wasn't long before the clank of the dismal chains followed the song. As the group passed by, Annie ventured a chance to raise her head and sneak a peek at the inmates. Jay was at the end of the line. How had he managed that, she wondered? Concentrating, she telegraphed a message to him. *I'm here. We've come for you.*

The guard closest to Jay had been at the site of the lynching. She would not soon forget his soulless eyes. He was no more than twenty feet from her when the group came to a halt.

Further up the road at the house, Troy Raines's wagon stopped, and he made his way up to the porch to greet Joshua. Not waiting for an invitation, he dropped into one of the oversized cane rocking chairs. Ann and Emma came out of the house carrying trays with lemonade and cookies right on cue.

"Evening, Mr. Raines," welcomed Ann. "Perhaps you might enjoy some of these cookies I baked with your lemonade. It's right warm for April, wouldn't you say?"

Indifferent to Ann's pleasantries, Raines grunted back. "Where's Missouri this evening"?

"She's tending to Mamie and her new baby. A little girl came last night."

Raines had no interest in small talk with Ann and greeted Joshua.

Resting at the bottom of the steps was a cistern filled with water. As Young Josh approached the porch carrying an armload of wood, the elder Joshua spoke first to Emma. "Gal, get a bucket and haul some water out to Mr. Raines's men." Then addressing Josh, he added, "boy, put that wood down and help her. Ann's right. It's hot out here."

"Take some cookies too," added Ann. I made plenty."

Josh rushed around to the side of the house, grabbing a bucket and ladle. After filling the bucket, the two children cautiously headed down the road to the men guarding the prisoners. Each man drank from the scoop and accepted cookies from Emma. At the house, the front door flew open, and two boys ran out laughing and bumping into Josh's chair and the table holding the pitcher of lemonade knocking everything over. Joshua jumped to his feet, nostrils flaring; he raged at the boys for their clumsiness. Raines shook his head with contempt. Guards and prisoners were predictably distracted by the commotion.

Annie sprinted from her hiding place, holding tight to their possession in the bend of her elbow and grabbing Jay's hand with her free hand. Emma and Josh quickly backed into Jay, Josh grabbed his other hand, and Emma held tightly to Josh to make sure all four were connected. A startled guard caught sight of the group and shouted at them, but his reaction was too slow. As he and the others reached for their guns, Annie smirked at both Raines and Joshua Calhoun.

Raines's eyes bulged as his jaw dropped, but a brief reflection of satisfaction crossed Joshua Calhoun's face as he hooked his thumb in his belt loop.

"Now," she barked, and the four voices rang out in unison. "Sankofa."

Chapter 20

A Party for The Ages

The four gazed about bewildered to discover they'd returned to the shabby cabin in the year 1935. Annie recalled the vision in the mirror and surmised the journey was approaching its conclusion with the anniversary party. She reminded the others of Mamie's declaration that they would attend the party and described how two days before the museum's opening, there was an image in the mirror of them enjoying themselves at the celebration of Missouri and Joshua's fiftieth anniversary.

"This is our last stop before we go home though I haven't figured out why," Annie said.

"Well, I don't believe it's to meet the Unknown Ancestor," mocked Josh.

"The journey and the lessons it holds may be as significant as identifying the ancestor, if not more," said Jay. "I've learned plenty, and I'm not a part of your family. Think about it. Emma was furious that Annie brought her back, but being here in the past, she found the courage to pursue her future aspirations. Now, she will approach her dance studies with a new level of confidence and determination. The Sankofa legend teaches us to scrutinize our history to understand our origins. That's how we move toward our destinies. The elders reminded Emma that she comes from resilient stock. We all do."

"You're taking this pretty well, considering you ended up on the chain gang," said Josh.

"Talking to those guys on the chain gang was eye-opening. I understand even more about the justice and penal system in our own time. It's not new; it's steeped in the country's history. Being a lawyer is something I have often considered; now, I am certain I want to pursue a legal career. When I do, it will be with the understanding that our people and the poor suffered from a system stacked against them. It has to change, and I want to be a part of that change."

Interrupted by the uncontrollable giggles of Missouri and Claudia, they were elated the two ladies were sitting in the same place they'd left them when Sankofa transported them to 1923. Missouri was still telling stories about her family and the mysterious Sankofa bird. Her breath hitched from laughter as she relayed the account of the day following the birth of her granddaughter Alone.

"Lemonade spilled all over the porch, but the boys were careful to make sure none got on Raines. Then, those visiting children surrounded their friend and yelled out the name of that strange bird.

The wind kicked up, and before everyone's eyes, poof, the kids were gone. I am sure they just rolled down the hill and high-tailed it out of there. But Ann set out to distract Troy Raines and his men. She got to jumping up and down, eyes rolling all-around in her head, screaming, 'Lord, they's hanks.' Joshua threw up his hands and began shouting and praying in tongues, though if I had to swear to it, I would say Joshua was play-acting. I recognized the mischief in his eyes even if Raines didn't.

Then, the prisoners started shouting and praying. I swear I've never seen such a stir. Raines's men were so scared; I half expected them to clear out. Raines commenced to yelling for them to go after those youngins, but the kids had vanished. I was peeking out the window, which was a good thing because I was laughing as hard then as I am now. If Raines had seen me, he would have guessed we had made a fool of him."

As their laughter died down, Claudie angled her baffled face toward Missouri. "You said you think the children got away by rolling down the hill, but how did they remove the chain and shackle off their friend's ankle"?

Missouri gazed into the distance, eyes blazing with the implausible memory of that day. In place of answering Claudia's question, Missouri patted her friend's knee and chuckled. "I should head back to the house and make certain all is ready."

The four children followed Missouri at a discreet distance. Their clothing changed as was customary to align with the era and circumstance, so it was no surprise party clothes were the order of the day. Emma was period-classic in a peach muslin cotton dress with a white collar and lace embroidery around the puffed sleeves and hemline. Annie's dress was two-toned with a dark green smocked bodice and a lighter green pleated skirt. Jay and Josh wore white buttoned shirts and high-waisted, wide-legged pants. Jay nudged Annie.

"I could start a whole new trend if I wore this to the school dance. What do you think?"

Annie blushed, recalling how desperate she'd been to be with Jay at the Fall dance. The adventures of the past few days outweighed the significance of the dance. Twice over three months, she'd traveled through time. She returned to the present a different person after the first experience. This occurrence already had an impact, undoubtedly with more to come. How would school dances fit in after witnessing lynchings, chain gangs, and the complicated birth of an ancestor by a Cherokee shaman, who happened to be another ancestor? *Mom will have a field day writing about all of this.*

"You're remarkable confident of starting a trend rather than becoming a laughingstock," she teased.

Glancing around, she realized it had been barely an hour since the daring escape from the Calhoun property, but twelve years had passed since the birth of Alone. Little had changed at the dwelling, but it had mellowed over the years, and the landscape's maturity showed. It was not yet spring, but the white oak trees dotting the property were taller and fuller with hints of blooms that would sprout in the coming weeks. In the distance, a few houses sat where none had been when they left. Annie inhaled, absorbing her surroundings. Despite her birth in 2003 and her leap through the generations, she felt she belonged here. This land was the dawn of the McElmurry-Calhoun story of freedom; she would paint that story forever as a daughter of that history.

Someone had placed chairs around the yard, and the four parked themselves to observe the festivities. Annie reached in her bag for her sketch pad and commenced drawing. The stately home was the focal point of her first sketch. Then she concentrated on capturing people as they arrived. The call of familiar names echoed across the yard, Cicero and Isabella greeting Noah and Lavonia. The anticipation of Emma coming from Ohio with her husband, Howard Calloway, was celebrated by her siblings.

The jubilant mood was contagious. Emma, Jay, and Josh relaxed and enjoyed the unseasonably warm February weather. There was live music playing, and the smell of a roasting pig wafted in the breeze. As the number of guests grew, Annie dared to approach the front door to glimpse inside the house. Joshua and Missouri were posing for a formal picture to commemorate the occasion. Often, Annie viewed this picture featuring Joshua sitting with Missouri standing on his right, resting her hand on his shoulder. She scribbled details on her pad that had faded from photos over the years. She was committed to painting a portrait of this scene, and now she had details to improve upon the photograph cherished by her family.

Studying her ancestors, she almost missed the presence of someone approaching. Glancing over her shoulder was Mamie standing behind her. She was different from the exuberant young girl Annie first met, but her kindness and warmth were still present. Mamie struggled a bit with her words as she extended her hand, holding a green ribbon. "This matches your dress. May I bind it in your hair?" Before Annie responded, Mamie reached over and tied the ribbon in her hair.

It was lopsided and loosely tied, but to Annie, it was perfect. "Thank you."

Standing at the threshold, Annie recalled the image of this day reflected in her mirror. Mamie in the doorway, just as she had observed. Emma and Josh were playing with other kids, and the unidentified person she'd seen surveilling them turned out to be Jay.

Little wonder he was familiar to her in the apparition; Jay's destiny was *to travel. The Unknowns planned it that way before the day at the museum.*

Annie chuckled and murmured, "The moment you doubt whether you can fly, you cease forever to be able to do it.'"

"J.M. Barrie, Peter Pan," Mamie quietly stated and walked away.

Mouth agape, Annie mentally dissected Mamie's words and their meaning. Since their initial meeting, where Mamie eagerly anticipated her future teaching career and plans to include Barrie's Peter Pan in her curriculum, Annie had read the work multiple times and quoted from it. Regardless of the mental treasures lost to Mamie during Alone's birth, her memory and affection for the tale of the boy who would never grow up remained. That suggested other comprehension persisted as well. Grief pieced Annie's heart. She pictured what could have been if her great-great-grandmother had received proper treatment during and after her pregnancy.

"Bedeviled McElmurrys," echoed the gruff voice behind her.

Annie pivoted and grinned at Joshua Calhoun. "Congratulations on your anniversary."

Joshua bent his elbow, offering it to Annie. She looped her arm through his, and the pair descended the stairs and walked away from the house.

They strolled in a peaceful silence until Joshua finally spoke. "Missouri tried to brush off what happened the day you children left, but I knew better. She wasn't aware her father told me a story of descendant children who went back and forth through time. He said preserving the truth of our people, and his family especially was their duty. Once Missouri became my family, he believed I should be aware of the unusual burden the Almighty had placed on his family. However, he didn't tell me until he was ready to leave this earth.

Fox was old, and I figured his mind was going the way old folks' minds go. I didn't think much more about it until there you were when Alone was born. Folk think I don't pay much attention to children, but I know who comes and goes in my house, and I had never seen you or the others before. Besides that, everything about you was different from any youngin I ever knew. Way too much sass in the presence of elders. Is that what they do where you're from?"

He didn't wait for an answer.

"I don't know what to think about you children, but I know folk are not supposed to know about what's to come in the future. So, you and the others need to go on back now. Carry your secrets about my children and grandchildren with you. You may not plan to tell what you know, but on the night Alone was born, when emotions were high, it just came out. That could happen again with more serious consequences."

Joshua's words stung. They were planning to leave when the party ended, but he didn't want them there at all. Annie wanted to say something to defend their right to stay or to return, but she realized whatever words uttered in their defense would prove his point. She would be revealing something about her relationship to him or something about the future, and he believed all of that should remain hidden.

Instead, she questioned why he considered the McElmurry capacity for time-traveling a burden?

"It's not so much the time-traveling," he responded. "It's the responsibility to reconstruct the lost history of a people and to right the wrong of deceitful tales."

Annie bobbed her head, signaling her understanding. She had concluded as much herself, believing an inability to identify the Unknown Ancestor would constitute a massive failure on her part. Her expression must have revealed her unspoken regrets because Joshua's face softened. "You are not the first, and I reckon you won't be the last. It is a puzzle where each generation holds a tiny piece. Be honored the Ancestors chose you for a part in that colossal task.

After extending her hand to shake with Joshua, she gestured to the others to join her.

"You should go down the road a piece, so you don't scare anyone when you vanish." He scrutinized each one. "I shouldn't ask, but since I know one name, I might as well be familiar with the rest of you."

"I'm Emma."

"My name is Jay. I'm not family, just a friend."

"The way she went after me when Raines grabbed you, I think Annie here feels a bit more than friendship."

"What is it with everyone" blushed a mortified Annie?

Josh hesitated before responding to the man whose name he bore. "I'm Joshua."

The elder Joshua stared at the young boy for a long time and nobly nodded his head. Waving them down the road lined with stately oak trees, he whispered, "Time to move on now."

Annie dug into her bag and pulled out the sculpture that launched their journey and would now take them home. She peeped around her shoulder to where Joshua remained standing in the road, observing them as they departed. Fire would one day destroy the Calhoun manor, but for now, it was visible at a distance, a splendid testament to Missouri and Joshua's accomplishments. Joshua's three descendants and their friend would forever remember his signature inscrutable gaze as they made their way down the road.

"He's probably making sure we leave," Annie mumbled.

"Maybe. Or maybe he's memorizing every detail to rekindle this image when he thinks about all of you and what the future holds for his descendants," said Jay.

"Perhaps," he continued, "the reason you had to make the last stop is to heed Joshua's message. You can't tell people in the past what you know about the future, even the good things. I agree with Joshua Think what people would do to try and change the outcome of history if they had an inkling of what is to be. Joshua may not endorse time travel, but he has to be proud of his legacy."

"I told Fox about President Obama," Annie proudly declared.

For whatever reason, they all found that very funny and doubled over with laughter.

The four caught hands. Annie and Jay book-ended the group; Josh and Emma were in the middle. Annie thrust her free arm in the air and arched the small statue over her head. "Ready, guys?"

"Ready."

Chapter 21

Home Again Home Again

The young voyagers of time travel popped inside the museum, at the entrance of the Freedom House exploding with shouts of joy. Jay and Josh high-fived. Emma twirled and posed in arabesque. Squealing in delight, Annie wrapped her arms around herself and tapped her feet up and down.

"What do you think you are doing?"

Flushed with embarrassment and struggling to gain composure, the four rebounded from their excitement and faced Sophia Sesstry.

Poised to launch into a stern lecture on proper etiquette in the museum, Sophie paused gapping at her curly-headed daughters and spotted the tattered green ribbon in Annie's hair. Though time-worn, the ribbon survived the journey of over ninety years. Rubbing the piece of fabric between her fingers, Sophie directed her attention to the shimmering expression in her daughter's eyes as the realization of what had transpired crystallized. Annie's trembling hand covered Sophie's as she grasped the presence and significance of the ribbon appearing in her time.

Sophie inspected the two younger children.

"You remember this time." It was a statement, not a question uttered by Sophie.

Josh and Emma nodded enthusiastically.

"We remember the first trip now, too, added Josh."

Shifting her attention to Jay, Sophie persisted in her questioning. "And Am I to assume you went along?"

"Yes, ma'am."

Focusing again on Annie, Sophie continued quizzing her daughter. "How long were you there?"

"Two days, I think. But we bounced back and forth, so it's hard to be certain."

Sophie fought for self-control, though she was terrified by the idea of her children spending two days alone in the past in the segregated South. She had been with them barely thirty minutes earlier; now, she was confronting a repeat supernatural experience she would be unable to describe to most of her friends and family.

"Who did you encounter? Wait, never mind. We don't have time to go into this now. And this is not the appropriate place for the conversation we will want to have. Tomorrow, we will discuss what happened. Besides, your grandmother would be irritated if we left her out.

Annie, you can invite Jay to the hotel with your friends tonight while Dad and I attend the gala."

Jay jumped in. "Thanks, Mrs. Sesstry, but I have plans."

"I'm not surprised, considering how involved your family has been with the museum. I will call your parents tomorrow and invite them over and take a crack at an explanation of our unusual family and how you became tangled up this adventure."

Sophie paused, mentally struggling to describe her family's experience over several generations and how she could possibly explain it to outsiders.

As if reading her mother's mind, "Bedevilment," teased Annie as her mouth twisted into a smirk. Amused by her mother's puzzled expression, she added, "I'll explain later."

"If you don't mind, Mrs. Sesstry, Jay said, I would rather you not have that conversation with my parents. It would require describing the experience, and my mom would probably freak if I told her I'd been captured and held on the chain gang. And you have to admit, all of this is hard to believe."

A massive headache ambushed Sophie, compelling her to massage her temples with the tips of her fingers.

Jay spotted his mother across the room. "Speaking of which, there's my mom. I should catch up with her." He offered Josh a fist bump and kissed Emma on the cheek. He then flashed Annie that belly-twisting grin. "Catch you at school."

"Yeah, talk to you later, Annie casually returned."

Annie spent Sunday dinner recounting the details of their most recent experience. Emma and Josh added their input and described what they remembered from the first encounter. Sophie's stomach churned listening to the tale of her baby's kidnapping the previous summer. At the tender age of thirteen, Annie witnessed a lynching. Her friend was a prisoner on the chain gang. She understood Jay's reluctance to inform his parents about the experience.

John and Sophie decided against talking to the Anders for the time being, but there would come a time when they would relay the story. They had a parental obligation. One thing was sure. Under no circumstances would their children be allowed to travel back in time again. John confiscated the Sankofa carving for safekeeping.

Annie didn't need her parents to object to further time travel. She was lukewarm to future visits to the past. Most of what she and the others had learned on this expedition shattered her fantasies about her ancestors. They were no closer to identifying the Unknown Ancestor than they had been before the last foray. Taking another trip was pointless since she had not figured out what, where, or when to find the next clue to their genesis in this country. Furthermore, Joshua made it clear they didn't belong in the past, and he didn't want any of them there.

John agreed with Sophie that it was too dangerous for the children to travel to the past again. But he explained how important it was for Annie to understand that recognizing the flaws in people, specifically Joshua, didn't diminish his accomplishments or his love for his family. Joshua was only trying to protect the people he loved under the most challenging circumstances. To have time travelers visit from the future only complicated matters more. She shouldn't judge a 1920s man by 2016 standards. He was an honest and decent man and attained remarkable achievements for the times with the help of a strong Black woman.

After three days and no word from Jay, Annie assumed she'd misread their experience together. They'd bonded through a precarious and extraordinary situation. Now things were back to normal, he had his regular friends, and he'd forgotten about her. He probably wasn't interested in her at all. Jay was one of the most popular boys in school, and she was the girl with the weird name – Ann Sesstry. What did she expect? She expected him to at least call, that's what.

Annie was startled when Jay ran up behind her on Wednesday morning and draped his arm around her shoulders as she was going to her locker.

"Hey, you said my phone would reemerge."

"Hello to you too."

"Sorry, I've been so frustrated over the last few days. I've been all over school searching for you. I wanted to call, but I never found my phone. I would have asked Kirsten to give you a message, but she hasn't been to swim practice. I finally found out the location of your locker and figured I would hang out until you showed up.

Anyway, I have a lot to tell you. First, I found something for you." Reaching in his backpack, Jay pulled out a photocopy of an old newspaper obituary of Joshua Calhoun.

Annie couldn't believe he was still interested in her family search after they'd returned to their own time. She read the glowing account of her ancestor's life from the *Macon Telegraph*, January 24, 1937. Joshua died short of three years after his fiftieth wedding anniversary.

"My deepest sympathies," Annie wisecracked.

"He was a cool dude, Annie. It's not abnormal to doubt him, to be angry about how he reacted. But considering the times, he managed better than many others in that era. He managed with the help of Missouri."

"My dad expressed a similar opinion."

"Also, Mr. Hennessy's talked about the opening of the museum in history class and how it's encouraging people to learn more about Black history in general and their own family story as well. He's going to arrange a field trip for our class. I could conduct the tour for him, but I didn't say that. But after class, I spoke to him about Fox, and your family's research into him and how that's as far back as your family could go. He said that's better than many families, Black or White can do. But he had another theory. He questioned if Fox was more than a nickname. Before his Virginia slavers sold him, it might have been a surname in Virginia. He wondered if he could have been Laverne Fox and not Laverne McElmurry until he went to Georgia to a different slaveholder.

Mr. H was curious about his theory, so he did some rudimentary research and found an enslaved kid named Laverne Fox in Amherst, Virginia.

"He was one of several enslaved in a batch sold to Georgia slave traders around the time your family has Fox showing up in Georgia. The Virginia Museum of History & Culture in Richmond has an extensive collection on the Virginia slave trade and may have more details. I was wondering if maybe one Saturday, you and I could catch a bus down there and conduct some research."

Annie wasn't sure what thrilled her more, the possibility of discovering additional information on Fox's history and the Unknown Ancestor or that Jay wanted to travel with her to Richmond to search for clues. Both unanticipated developments brightened her mood as things were about to improve even more.

Jay hitched his backpack on his shoulder. "I have to get to class, but I'll talk to you later about Richmond."

He started walking, then swung around. "One more thing. My folks and some other parents are renting a party bus for the fall dance. Do you think your parents will let you ride with us?"

It was Annie's turn to respond coyly as a playful grin tickled the sides of her mouth. "I think there's a good chance, that is, as long as we stay in the current century."

Epilogue

Four hundred years have lapsed since ships of oppression carried guiltless people from the land of their birth to a hostile territory and a prison of grief. Throughout the generations, in chains, we gazed at the same moon and stars as those we left to mourn our absence, gazed in freedom. We gave birth in hope to children conceived in hopelessness. All the while, we persevered. It is this fountain of faith that sustains us. It assures us of victory.

The wisdom of the ancestors teaches, "Knowledge is a garden. If it isn't cultivated, it cannot be harvested." The Unknowns have and will continue to plant the seeds of Knowledge. It is the responsibility of future generations to nurture and cultivate the garden to yield rich crops at the gathering time. The fruits of the harvest are many; the perpetuation of a people, the beauty of the land, the appreciation of the history and the connection to something greater than ourselves. The lasting fruits of the harvest are the curious minds we cultivate in each generation to carry on the quest.

And thus, it is that the children will continue the work of the planters until our people have reached the zenith of their creation. The young have not been tainted by the malevolency of the need for power at any price. Caution them though, lest the quest seduces them. It is arrogance to assume that a single soul has been bestowed with the responsibility of unraveling the mystery of the ancestors alone. Indeed, that is the antithe-

sis of being connected to the tribe. Search for other tribal travelers as they have tales to tell.

There is more to the story. And there are other young people destined to share in the telling.

Acknowledgments

An old saying exists about the best-laid plans of people. I started this book three years ago, but life interrupted my goals, and the book's completion was delayed. The Book of Ecclesiastes states, "For everything, there is a season, A time for every purpose under heaven." In other words, things happen when they are supposed to. At the start of the Annie Sesstry series, I could not have imagined discussing elements of America's past, such as those addressed in Annie's adventures, could be banned in public schools.

There is strained debate on what books young people can and should read concerning race and the history of our nation; discussion on what divides and what unites. Critical Race Theory is the latest boogieman, ask three people on the street what it means, and you are guaranteed to get three different answers. Family, love, and friendship prevail even in the darkest of times. That is the core of the Sesstry series. Hopefully, these stores can contribute to the discussion of race positively.

My most profound appreciation for this book goes to my mother, Alone Jones Lilienthal, who retold the stories of her childhood, her unconditional love for her grandmother Missouri, and the challenges of growing up with a mother who suffered brain damage giving birth. My sister Marsha Lilienthal Boddie kept me focused on who is who in our lineage and pointed me in the right direction on family research.

Thank you, Eric and Shellie Anders, for allowing me to include your son EJ in my story as the charming and urbane Jay. He was fourteen when I started writing, and now, he is off to Morehouse in Georgia! I wish him much success in the future.

Carrie Jones, my developmental editor, made me a better writer with her advice and encouragement. Hannah VanVels Ausbury's copy edits were focused and put me in the position to bring this project to a close. Both women have helped me believe in myself as a writer and have inspired me to continue writing, not just about the McElmurry-Calhoun sagas, but to record the dozens of tales that have circled in my heart and head for years.

Finally, thanks as always to my husband, Clarke. No one could be blessed with a stronger or more loyal advocate. I could write volumes about his support but stating that he believes in me is enough.

A Few Things I learned along the Way:

In African lore, Sasha are spirits who are known to the living. At the passing of the last person to have personally known an elder, that elder leaves the Sasha to join Zamani, who are deceased spirits unknown to the living.

I found the words attributed to Henry McNeal Turner in the African Repository, volumes 51-53, July 1876, and in a letter written by Pastor Turner on February 22, 1883. The New Georgia Encyclopedia is an additional source of information on Turner, who also spent twelve years as the chancellor of Morris Brown College (now Morris Brown University), the Alma Mater of Mamie Calhoun Jones.

Moses McKissack was the founder of McKissack & McKissack, the first Black-owned architectural firm and the oldest minority/women-owned professional design and construction firm in the United States.

The book highlights Early Calhoun's service in World War I. Noah Calhoun senior also served in World War I, as did Aquilla Sr., who entered the military at 14.

The state of Georgia opened a public sanatorium in Banks County to treat tuberculosis in 1911. It was considered one of the most ambitious health projects in the nation when Joshua and Missouri credited the hospital for saving the life of their youngest child Lilla, in an era when tuberculosis was ravaging the country.

WT Anderson created the colored pages in the Macon Telegraph for Blacks. The Telegraph featured the obituary of Joshua Calhoun at the time of his death. Troy Raines sought permission from Missouri to attend the funeral.